IN THE NAME OF THE FATHER

Ms. Lisa,

Thanks

for your support!

God Bless!

Allyson

Olivia

12/3/14

1/12/15

IN THE
NAME
OF THE
FATHER

ALLYSON
OLIVIA

ISBNs: 978-0-9850217-0-2 (hardcover); 978-0-9850217-1-9 (paperback); 978-0-9850217-2-6 (eBook)

Library of Congress Control Number: 2014908075 Library of Congress Cataloging-in-Publication Data is on file at the Library of Congress, Washington, DC.

Published by Penvision Ink, LLC www.penvisionink.com

ACKNOWLEDGMENTS

Above all else, I thank my Lord and Savior, Jesus Christ, for giving me life. Lord, thank you for blessing me with the ability to dream. If I could write a million books and fill them with praise, it could never be enough to thank you for all you have done for me.

I thank my mom for believing in my dreams, even when I started to let them fade. Your love and support has shaped me into the woman I am today. I thank my brother for being excited about all my ideas and projects. I thank my father for loving me unconditionally. I also thank my family members and friends who have always encouraged me. Finally, to all who have helped me along the way, I want to thank you for this journey.

· · · · ·

Special Thanks
Corey Richburg, photographer — Cover Artwork
Tre'Lynn Photography — Back Cover Picture

DEDICATION

This work of fiction is dedicated to my husband. Thank you for loving me as described in 1 Corinthians 13:1–8. I pray our love will always protect, always trust, always hope, and always persevere. You love me like Christ loves the church, and I cannot ask for more.

In loving memory of Granny Willeen Shields. Your legacy will live in my heart forever. You meant so much to God that He took you from earth while you were dreaming. You are my angel.

In loving memory of Cousin Lisa and Aunt Fuzzy. Your love will always live in our hearts.

· · · · ·

This is dedicated to every person who has ever had to release their past to love in the present.

CHAPTER ONE

"I can't believe you're getting married in less than an hour," Pam said as she placed the short white veil on Angel's head to complement her hair styled into a large, neat chignon.

Angel paused and forced her lips to form a smile, but didn't say a word.

"Are you excited?"

"I think I'm making a mistake by marrying Lester," Angel admitted.

"Then don't marry him. I'll tell everyone at the church to go home and that there's nothing to see here."

"No, it's too late. We purchased a house and it would just be a mess to turn back now. I love him, but something hit me hard this morning as I prayed."

"What hit you?"

"I realized I never prayed about marrying Lester. I fell in love and went with the flow, but as I prayed this morning a feeling came over me like knots twisting in my stomach and I threw up."

"Maybe that's just cold feet."

"I don't know, but it will be okay. I love Lester and I'm sure things will only get better as we begin to spend our lives together, because this is until death do us part."

"Yeah, that's what I said when I got married the first time." Pam laughed as she dabbed Angel's face with pressed powder to reduce the shine from her perspiring skin.

"You're a mess, you know that? But that's why I love you and wouldn't have anyone else be my matron of honor."

As Angel stared in the mirror while Pam put the finishing touches on her makeup, she thought about the night she met Lester and how they got engaged.

Since Angel and her girlfriends wanted to listen to live music and dance the night away, they resolved to spend a Friday night on December 26, 1975, at the popular spot Tony's in downtown Baltimore.

"Looks like it's going to be a fun time. There's a good crowd tonight," Angel said as she surveyed the club to predict the chances of meeting a gentleman worth her time.

They found a table close to the bar and were seated for a few moments. Swaying and snapping her fingers to the band's smooth sound, tapping her feet to the beat, Angel couldn't sit still. She was ready to hit the dance floor.

"Listen up, everybody," the DJ announced. "We have a birthday boy in the house tonight. Everybody, put your hands together for my man Lester. Happy birthday, Lester."

After the announcement, Angel positioned herself to get a good look at the birthday boy in the spotlight. *He is one fine man*, Angel thought, then started swinging her hips to the music again. *Wonder where the good-looking birthday boy disappeared to?* Just as she began to scan the room for Lester, someone tapped her on the shoulder. Angel turned and tried not to smile as wide as her heart was pounding.

"You know it's my birthday, and that means you owe me a birthday dance," Lester said as he extended his hand toward Angel. "What's your name, beautiful?"

"Thank you. My name is Angel." She blushed and shook Lester's hand.

"That's a fitting name for a woman as stunning as you are, but I'm sure you hear that a lot."

"Thank you." Angel smiled.

"I noticed you when you arrived with your girlfriends, and I planned to get close enough to see if you were wearing a rock on your ring finger, or if it was bare and I had a chance to get to know you or at least have the honor of a dance."

"As you can see my ring finger is bare."

"May I have this dance, Angel?"

"You never told me your name." Angel smiled as she leaned in to hear this handsome man's name.

"Oh, I apologize. I thought you remembered it from the DJ wishing me a happy birthday. It's Lester."

"Okay, Lester, Mr. Birthday Boy, let's dance." Angel popped up from her stool like she had something to prove on the dance floor.

Lester took her hand as they walked onto the dance floor. The couple was picture-perfect as they danced the night away. Lester stood six-foot-two and weighed 185 pounds. His brown skin was smooth with only a neatly trimmed mustache to distract from his dark brown, piercing eyes. He was sharp from the top of his head to his wing-tip shoes.

Angel was average in stature, but she made up for her five-foot-five height by wearing three-inch stilettos. Her almond skin was like butter. It was accented with just enough makeup to illuminate her natural beauty. Her long black hair was twisted in a large cluster of curls neatly pinned up in a classic coiffure. Her dark brown, doe-like eyes were surrounded by long black lashes. Her luscious lips were coated with a deep-red lipstick hiding her white teeth until she smiled. She was also dressed to impress and everything was in place, from the pins in her hair to the fierce shoes that matched her dress. She didn't blend in with the crowd, but defined it.

"There is something different about you. I'm not sure what it is, but I like it. Can I see you again, Ms. Angel? What's your last name?" Lester asked when the music stopped and the emcee announced the club was shutting down.

As the lights blinked on and everyone adjusted their eyes to the bright room, Angel pulled away from Lester's chest where she had rested her head during the last slow song.

"It's Sword, and you can see me again, Mr. Lester." Angel grinned as she waited for Lester to reveal his last name.

"It's Noble."

"It would be Noble, wouldn't it?" Angel thought this was too good to be true.

"It is and I am. You can bet on that."

"Well, Mr. Noble, I'm not a betting woman, but I'll take your word for it."

"Oh, if you're not a betting woman, then what are you?"

"I'm saved, sanctified, and filled with the Holy Ghost. That beats a betting woman any day," Angel said as she scribbled her number on a napkin she'd grabbed from the bar buried behind the empty glasses and ashtrays piled high with cigarette butts.

"Ah, a Holy Roller who is fine and likes to dance, that's an interesting combination." Lester laughed as he happily took Angel's number.

"It was nice meeting you, Angel. I see your friends are waiting for you across the room by the exit to make sure you're okay, so I'll say goodnight."

"It was nice meeting you, too, Lester. Have a good night and be safe." Angel shook his hand and played down her excitement until she was out of Lester's sight.

When Angel and her friends got outside they immediately grilled her about Lester. They covered all the bases from his last name to his job. But the most important question was if she gave Lester her number. Now they would have to wait and watch their story unfold. In the car ride from the club, Angel replayed every moment from the encounter at least twenty times.

When Lester called the following Monday, the conversation between the two came easy. They didn't have to find things to discuss because they had everything to explore, since they were starting from scratch.

"Do you attend church?" Angel asked, praying Lester's answer would be yes. She didn't want to date anyone who wasn't living for God, but she already liked him and was hoping he wasn't an atheist because that was a deal breaker.

"I attend occasionally, but I've been meaning to go more

often. I know the Lord and I read the Bible. You don't have to worry your pretty self, I'm not a heathen."

"Lester, you know that's what all heathens say." Angel laughed at her own joke like she often did.

"That was funny. You got me."

Their chats were comforting to Angel and she began to let her guard down, though she never really had it up where Lester was concerned. Lester pulled out all the stops when they started dating. He sent long-stemmed roses to her job, left romantic notes on her car and cards on her doorstep, took her out to dinner almost every night, and lavished her with expensive gifts. His thoughtfulness combined with his gorgeous smile made Angel feel like she could spend the rest of her life with this man.

He had a promising career with the Department of Social Services as a social worker. He didn't have any children, had his own apartment, treated her like royalty, and said all the right things. The only thing that bothered Angel about Lester was his attempt to conceal his previous marriage.

She found out he was divorced six months after they'd started dating. Lester's older sister, Reese, pulled Angel aside one evening at dinner and told her she was too good for her brother. She shared that Lester was married before and made a mess of that relationship and ruined the woman's life. She warned her to leave Lester alone before it was too late. Angel always resented him for not sharing that information early on in their relationship, but she was head-over-heels in love by the time she found out and she wasn't turning back.

She wanted to spend the rest of her life as Mrs. Lester Noble. Lester also wanted to spend the rest of his life with Angel, although he never formally proposed. Instead of asking her father for his blessing and getting down on one knee, he just decided they were going to get married.

On Thanksgiving Day in 1976, he made an announcement to their family and friends that they were getting married. Angel was surprised and excited by the announcement because she hadn't had a clue. She wished Lester had proposed and presented her with an engagement ring before he announced it to everyone, but she cared more about getting married than the formalities.

Inhaling and exhaling slowly, Angel's chest went up and down as she breathed deeply, taking in her last few breaths as a single woman.

"Are you sure you want to go through with this?" Pam asked, interrupting her thoughts.

"Yes, I'm sure. Everyone is waiting. I'm ready." Angel stood in her plain, white knee-length dress and did a final look in the full-length mirror as Ms. Angel Sword. She added another bobby pin to the neatly positioned chignon at the nape of her neck and picked up the bouquet of fresh flowers bound by white satin ribbon.

The wedding was at an intimate Baptist church in Baltimore. Only relatives and close friends of the bride and groom were invited to the festive yet modest event. They were starting out with little money. Therefore, Angel didn't have an elaborate wedding dress like her four sisters who were married before her. As she walked down the narrow aisle of the church, her eyes met the eyes of the man who promised her the world.

"You may kiss the bride," the officiating minister announced to the fifty guests on July 25, 1977. Then he presented the couple as Mr. and Mrs. Noble. The newlyweds couldn't afford to go on a honeymoon or have a formal wedding reception, so they decided to receive guests in their new home. It was a house-warming and reception all rolled into one. After they ate, danced, and opened gifts, the newlyweds were forced to learn how to live together as one.

That night, in their bedroom, the chemistry was wrong. When Lester asked Angel to slip into one of the sexy outfits she received at her bridal shower, she was completely turned off. She didn't want to make love to her husband, and her gut told her she had made a costly mistake. The man who had swept Angel off her feet was not her soul mate. On their wedding night they didn't consummate their marriage; instead, they held each other until they dozed off from the draining excitement of their wedding day.

The next morning, Angel awoke to the smell of bacon and eggs. As she turned over in bed and opened her eyes she noticed a note on Lester's pillow. The note was folded and the front read: *To my Angel.* Angel picked up the note and read it slowly.

If love is forever, then we will be forever. The passion we have for each other will never fade. It will be so intense that our children will live their lives with a passion that can't be explained.

Angel smiled as she let out a sigh of relief. She attributed her lack of desire for her husband to nerves and fatigue, so she slipped into one of her negligees and surprised him in the kitchen.

CHAPTER TWO

The best thing that ever happened to him was marrying Angel. He longed for a loving wife and children, and a house he could call home. He wanted what some describe as the American dream. The American dream seemed like it would never come true for him until he met Angel.

Lester was the third youngest of fifteen brothers and sisters, ten of whom had the same mother and father; with the others he shared the same father. His mother was murdered by her boyfriend when he was nine. His father couldn't be bothered with raising any of his kids because that would infringe on his carefree lifestyle; consequently, he never took care of them. Lester's grandmother took care of him and three of his siblings for two years before she relinquished the responsibility because it was too burdensome. From that moment, Lester bounced between foster homes until he was eighteen. A smart boy, he always excelled in school and had an insatiable appetite for words. He read whatever he could get his hands on, including the Bible. He loved traveling mentally to different places, allowing words to distract him from the pains of life.

At eighteen, Lester enrolled in college and studied psychology. He was fascinated with the human mind and behavior. He thought if he helped other people work through their issues, somehow he would be cleansed from the skeletons in his closet.

He made an effort to release the pain of his childhood by working to be a better man daily. He treated people with respect and tried to shake the demon of depression that would creep into his thoughts when his mind wandered. Lester was relieved when he fell in love with Angel because she provided an escape from the life sentence of failure he carried with him. Though most people didn't see anything but confidence when they came in contact with Lester, he was unhappy. He never shared his feelings of failure with anyone because that would have made him weak. He smiled hard and always cracked jokes to distract from his disappointment with life.

When he connected with Angel it felt like she was his beacon of light. Angel was happy. She had something that Lester wished he had. He wasn't sure what she possessed, but it was illumination to the darkness of his soul. He vowed to always cherish her and hoped he would never extinguish her light. Since he was on his way to creating a better life for himself through being a family man, he took cues from how Angel's family loved each other.

Lester was attracted to Angel's drive and her commitment to family. He knew she would never leave him like many of the people he'd loved had. He thought his life couldn't get any better until he became a father.

Two years into the marriage, Lester and Angel rushed to the hospital late one evening, overwhelmed with the anticipation of their new baby.

"Don't forget the breathing techniques they taught you in class," Lester said as he mimicked one of the deep-breathing exercises.

"Just get us to the hospital safely, Les, and I'll worry about the breathing," Angel said as she squeezed Lester's hand, sharing the level of pain she was experiencing at the moment.

"Ouch, okay, I get the point. I will drive to the hospital in silence," Lester said as he pried his hand out of Angel's.

Lester drove like a madman all the way to the hospital, weaving in and out of lanes like he was in a police chase. He was nervous, but he tried to be strong for Angel. He didn't have a clue as to how to be a father, but he was determined to be the best dad he could be. When he pulled up to the emergency entrance he almost forgot to put the car in park and began to open his door.

"Don't forget to put the car in park," Angel yelled between deep breaths.

Walking into the hospital, Angel being admitted, and preparing for delivery were a blur for Lester. He was so excited he spent most of the time calling family and friends and telling everyone in the hospital his wife was in labor.

After being in labor for six hours, the doctor told Angel not to push, but she couldn't help it. Next thing Angel knew the doctor was shouting, "Wait!" and then he caught her bundle of joy like a football as he spun around on the small black stool. Lester felt faint after Angel went into labor. It could have been the excitement of the day, or the grip Angel had on his hand as she endured the pain of contractions. He kept it together for the delivery, and outside of the medical staff, Lester was the first person to lay eyes on his baby girl.

His daughter was born on the first day of spring in 1979. A few months before the birth, he and Angel decided to name her Grace Marie. However, once they saw the mole in the shape of a tear drop a few inches below her right eye, they decided to name her Joy. Lester said the mole was a tear of joy. When Lester held Joy in his arms he felt God was giving him a chance to experience true love. It was like God was showing him that the emptiness and pain of his childhood was dissolved in the eyes of this tiny baby. He cried, laughed, and experienced a flood of emotions while he thanked God for blessing him with a family. This moment in time was a rainbow. For Lester it reminded him of God's promise and purpose for his life. His passion for becoming who God designed him to be was pressing on his chest as he held Joy close. He didn't want to let her go.

"You are beautiful. You are going to be someone great. Thank you, God, for loving me enough to bless me with this life I hold in my arms. I won't take this responsibility for granted," Lester said as he held Joy and smiled.

Friends and family swarmed the hospital within an hour of

Joy Marie entering the world. Lester shook his head at Angel's obsession with her appearance, though that was one of the things that attracted him to her. He held Joy while he watched Angel curl her hair, put on makeup, and slip into a new pink silk robe before any visitors arrived. He couldn't believe after giving birth just a short while ago that she mustered up the energy to get dolled up, but he was learning that was his Angel. Their friends and family couldn't believe how great she looked right after giving birth. Lester could tell Angel loved all the attention she was getting as she soaked up every compliment before she was released from the hospital, though Joy managed to steal some of the attention away from Angel.

Joy was a seven-pound doll. Like most newborn babies, she was extremely pale. Her eyes were almond shaped like Lester's, and dark brown. She had a head full of dark brown hair.

Lester was so enthusiastic that he never wanted to release his little girl from his chest. Angel had to practically force him to put Joy down and get ready for work every day. She didn't want him to spoil Joy since Angel was the one at home with her while he worked. When Lester was at home he insisted on feeding and changing Joy. He loved being a father and he wanted to make sure he was doing everything right. He didn't have a step-by-step guide, but he knew if he was always there to help he would discover the right path. He prepared breakfast for Angel before he went to work and cleaned the house when he returned. There was no chore too great or small for Lester. If something had to be done, he was there.

Since Lester joined Mountain Hospital's staff as a social worker before Joy was born, they received diapers and formula for free. The new parents didn't have to worry about spending a lot of money on those items, which was a relief.

Lester wished he made more money to make it possible for Angel to stay home with Joy for a couple years, but his income wasn't enough to support them. When Angel went back to work, Lester continued to help out as much as he could around the house. He wasn't the best cook, so Angel did most of the cooking, but he helped with laundry and, of course, tending to Joy. Angel never had to ask for Lester's help when it came to Joy. When Joy was a few months old, Lester would pack a couple diapers and bottles and disappear for hours, showing off his little girl to all his friends and family. Lester knew Angel was thankful for the rest she got when he and Joy had their daddy-daughter time. He hoped Angel wouldn't become overwhelmed with working full-time and being a wife and mother, but observed it was a draining balancing act.

Lester's admiration of and attraction to Angel grew stronger after Joy was born. He couldn't keep his hands off his beautiful wife. He still planned dinners out on the town and sent elaborate bouquets of roses to her job to keep their romance fresh. He didn't want their passion to wither like flowers that are never watered. He prayed their love would blossom.

On one of their nights out, Lester was excited to take Angel to a new restaurant in downtown Baltimore at the Inner Harbor.

"What a breathtaking view of the harbor," Angel said as she glanced at the menu.

"It is nice. Only the best for my Angel." Lester noticed that Angel looked exceptionally radiant.

"I can't believe Joy is almost one, can you?" Angel asked as she reached across the table and covered Lester's hands with hers.

"I know our little girl is growing quickly. I want to freeze every moment, so I won't miss anything." Lester held Angel's hands tightly.

"I think Joy's going to be a great big sister." Angel leaned closer to Lester and placed his hands on her stomach.

"I knew you were glowing more than normal. You're beautiful and I'm blessed to be your husband. I love you."

"I love you, too, Les." Angel leaned into Lester and kissed him gently on the lips. "You think Joy is ready to share the spotlight?"

"I don't know about that, but she'll come around. We'll have to ease her into being a big sister. I hope it's a boy."

"I hope it's a boy, too."

"What will we name him?" Angel asked.

"I like Moses. He's going to be a leader." Lester beamed as he caressed Angel's cheek, looking up and thanking God for this moment.

· · · · ·

As the pregnancy progressed, Joy would speak to Angel's stomach. "When you come out, I'm in charge. You hear?" Joy demanded as she pressed her face into Angel's large belly.

Lester and Angel laughed when she went on a tirade and hoped when the baby was born, Joy would calm down.

Moses was born on July 4, 1981, and the summer heat and humidity made Angel very uncomfortable toward the end of her pregnancy. Moses didn't shoot out like Joy; instead, he wanted to take his time in making his arrival. As a result, the doctor did a C-section because he was in a rush and Moses didn't want to come out. Moses was pale, chubby, and hairy when he made his grand entrance into the world. Lester called all their family and friends and stopped everyone in the hospital and told them he was the proud father of a new baby boy. Just when Lester thought he had everything he wanted, there was a special bond formed when he saw Moses. As with Joy, he realized his responsibility to protect him. Even more, he realized he was Moses's example of manhood. He vowed to be there for him as his father and example. Lester was living his dream. His family was complete.

CHAPTER THREE

Joy didn't calm down once Moses was born and was often punished because she was too rough with her little brother. She insisted on pulling rank, even though he was just an infant.

Several months after Moses was born, Angel's father died of natural causes. After his death Lester and Angel packed up the family, sold their townhome, and moved in with Angel's mom, whom everyone affectionately called Gran. They thought moving in with Gran would help her adjust and assist them with saving money for a single-family home in Baltimore County. Years after Gran and her husband moved into the row house where they rented the top floor, they purchased the property and expanded into the rest of the house. The dwelling was still small, but if nine people could live there, Gran and the Noble family would be fine.

Initially, Joy and Moses shared a room, which was fine until Moses started walking and talking. Moses and Joy competed for their parents' attention from the day Moses was born. Both children especially competed for their father's attention. Joy was a daddy's girl and since she was the oldest, she thought Moses should follow her lead. She didn't like sharing with her little brother, whether it was a toy or her parents' affection.

After picking up the children from school and daycare, like usual, Lester dropped Joy, age five, and Moses, age three, off at home in Gran's care instead of letting them ride along to get Angel from work. When they arrived at home, Moses went upstairs and Joy ran into the kitchen to find out what Gran was cooking.

"Hi, Gran." Joy wrapped her arms around her waist, while Gran stirred pasta in a large metal pot. "When can we eat?" Joy asked as she tugged at Gran's floral apron.

"In about fifteen minutes, but you have to change your clothes and wash your hands first."

Joy ran upstairs to see what Moses was up to, but he wasn't in their bedroom or Gran's bedroom. Moses often hid from Joy and she thought he was probably trying to start a game of hide-and-seek. Joy crept down the hallway to her parents' room and slowly opened the door. Joy turned ten different colors and her jaw dropped as she stood speechless in the doorway. Moses, who barely talked, was sitting on the floor with a pair of scissors in hand, while chunks of his curly, sandy-brown hair covered the carpet.

Joy burst into the room and grabbed the scissors from him. "What did you do? You are in a lot of trouble, mister."

Moses didn't say a word. He just sat there, shrugging his little shoulders. Joy ran downstairs, yelling for Gran to see what Moses did. Gran slowly climbed the stairs to take inventory of the situation.

"Joy, why did you do this to your brother?"

"I didn't do this. When I came upstairs I found him like this."

"Sure you did," Gran said. "There is no way he could have cut his hair and not hurt himself. He's only three. Joy, go sit in the dining room until your parents come home."

Joy sat still at the dining room table in the large wooden dining-room chair, waiting for what seemed like her last meal. To Joy, it felt like days passed before Angel and Lester got home. When she heard the keys jingle in the lock, she bolted to the door to tell her side first.

"Mom, Dad, when I went upstairs I found Moses in your room with scissors in his hand. He cut all his hair off."

"What?" they chimed.

Then the little Edward Scissorhands bopped in. "Hi, Mom; hi, Dad. Look at what Joy did to my hair."

Joy was shocked by how talkative Moses was since he rarely

spoke. Lester and Angel took one look at his patchy head and couldn't believe this was their son.

"What happened to him? Joy, why did you do this?" they demanded with their arms folded.

Joy didn't have a defense. No one believed Moses could cut his own hair.

"We're relieved nobody was hurt, but do you realize how dangerous this was, Joy?" Angel asked as she rubbed Moses' patches on his head and cringed.

"It's almost funny when you think about it. I mean, Moses' head is a mess." Lester started to chuckle until Angel elbowed him in the stomach.

"Lester, this isn't a laughing matter. Let's not make light of what happened. We're glad both of you are okay, but I'm sure your father is going to punish you, Joy. Right, Les?"

"Joy, I can't believe you would be so irresponsible as to cut Moses's hair. Someone could have been seriously hurt with the scissors. You can't go outside and play or watch television for a week," Lester said.

"A week! But I didn't do anything. I didn't cut his hair. Moses is telling a fib," Joy cried out.

"Joy, on top of all this you have the nerve to call Moses a liar. Go to your room until we call you for dinner." Lester pointed upstairs.

Joy stomped upstairs, crying about the mess she was in at no fault of her own. She threw herself on her bed and buried her head in the pillow, mad at the world, especially Moses. Moses decided to follow Joy to their room and rub in his huge victory.

"Isn't it funny how nobody believes you?" Moses mocked.

· · · · ·

Like most parents, Lester and Angel wanted the best education for their children. When Joy was old enough to attend elementary school, they enrolled her at St. Peter's in Baltimore City. It was a huge, private Catholic school for primary grade levels slapped in the middle of prostitution and poverty. Joy often wondered why she went to a Catholic school since her family was Baptist, but when she asked her parents about it they told her it was best.

Typically, Lester dropped Joy off at school in the morning and picked her up from the after-school program in the evening. He would wait in his car at the bottom of the hill where he watched Joy walk into the auditorium for general attendance and morning announcements. One morning Lester kissed Joy goodbye and watched to see her make it up the hill safely.

"Love you, sweetie," Lester yelled as Joy ran up the hill, her book bag bouncing with every step.

"Love you, too," Joy yelled without turning around as she continued her sprint.

Dressed in a navy blue plaid jumper, a light blue collared shirt, navy blue sweater, and black-and-white string-up shoes, Joy normally blended in with the other female students when she walked into the auditorium, but this morning she was late.

"Hey, Joy!" An older boy smiled as Joy made it to the top of the hill.

"Hi," Joy mumbled as she kept walking toward the auditorium.

"Can I talk to you for a minute, cutie?"

"No, I'm in a hurry."

"You not in that big a hurry," he said as he waved his friend over.

"Give me a kiss," the boy demanded as he and his friend cornered Joy against a cement wall.

"Leave me alone or I'll…" Joy yelled at the top of her lungs with her hand on her hip.

"You'll what? Call for your daddy? Well, he ain't here."

Just as he leaned in to steal a kiss, Lester grabbed the boy by his collar and held him with one hand. The boy squirmed, with his feet dangling a few inches off the ground, while his friend started backing away slowly to stage a clean getaway.

"I'm gonna say this one time. If I catch you anywhere near my daughter, you will not live to tell anybody about it. Do you understand me?" Lester yelled as he dropped the boy to the ground.

He and his friend ran off from the parking lot like lightning was striking their heels and forming dust from the cold concrete.

"Thanks, Dad. That boy was trying to kiss me. He's in a higher grade," Joy said as she hugged Lester tightly around his stomach.

"Did he put his hands on you?" Lester asked as he crossed his arms.

"Well, he cornered me against the wall, but he didn't touch or kiss me. You came just in time."

"Nobody better ever put their hands on you. If they do you make sure you tell me. I wait at the bottom of the hill and watch you go inside the auditorium every morning, and I got worried when you weren't at the door. Alright, I'm sure he won't mess with you again. Have a good day and I'll pick you up later. Don't mention this to your mom. I don't want to upset her. Love you."

"Love you, too. I'm sure nobody will mess with me now." Joy winked at Lester then went inside the auditorium.

The buzz of Lester roughing up Joy's schoolmate traveled before Joy sat down in the auditorium. Joy liked all the attention she was getting at school because of Lester. She thought her father was invincible and now so did her classmates.

When Lester picked Joy up from the after-school program that evening, kids ran up to him and shook his hand. They lined up to greet him and give him dap. Lester heard a chorus of "Hi, Mr. Noble" from the time he picked Joy up until they got into the car.

Searching for ways to expose his children to new things, Lester took Moses and Joy to the Enoch Pratt Free Library located on Pratt Street in downtown Baltimore. The library, once a cathedral, was the largest public library in the city.

"Dad, why are we at the library?" Joy asked while pulling her father toward the exit. "I'm ready for dinner."

"I want you two to understand the importance of reading. You shouldn't watch a lot of television, but instead should be reading."

"But we like watching television," Joy responded for herself and Moses as she often did.

"I am going to show you and Moses how to check out library books. We are going to start coming here every week so you can check out two books and read them. Knowledge is something that can never be stolen from you. Your thoughts will only be cultivated more if you expose yourself to other worlds. Do you understand why this is important?"

Joy nodded her head like she understood what Lester meant, but she didn't have a clue. She just wanted to eat dinner and see Angel and Gran at home.

As he promised, Lester took Joy and Moses to the library once a week. He helped them with their homework and read for the few minutes they didn't require his undivided attention. In addition to the library, Lester took them to baseball games, professional wrestling matches, amusement parks, the circus, and restaurants when they had free time.

On one excursion, Lester took Joy, Moses, and their cousins Joshua, Jay, and Kira to hop rocks at a nearby stream. They hopped from rock to rock over the water, making sure to keep their balance, then took a break to rest up. Everyone was talking when they heard someone cry out.

"Help! Help me! I'm gonna fall, Daddy."

"Where is Moses?" Joy yelled, wondering what he'd gotten himself into now.

Joy frantically ran close to a nearby cliff and heard Moses yelling loudly while his small hands held on for life with his eyes closed tightly and face pointed to the sky.

Joy ran to Lester and pulled him toward the cliff. "Dad, help! Moses slipped down a waterfall and is hanging on the side of a cliff."

"Daddy, help! Help me! Daddy!" Moses cried out while gripping the side of the cliff. His tiny hands started to bleed. He continued to yell while tears fell from his eyes and snot dripped from his nose.

"I'm coming, Moses. Hold on," Lester yelled as he ran toward Moses's voice.

Joy watched as Lester knelt down at the edge of the cliff and extended his long arm down, pulling Moses up by his shirt. Joy and her cousins jumped for Joy when Lester brought Moses to safety. Joy stood behind Lester, waiting for him to yell at Moses for being clumsy again, but he didn't lecture Moses about wandering off and almost falling to his demise. Instead he put him over his shoulder and hugged him tightly.

"I love you," Lester said as he wiped tears from his own eyes while he carried Moses to the car. "Are you okay?"

"I'm okay." Moses still looked terrified and didn't say anything else while he rested on Lester's broad shoulder.

"Thank God you're okay. I don't know what I would have done if I'd lost you." Lester pressed him into his chest. "I pray your mom doesn't find out about this."

"What happened to you guys? You're covered in dirt!" Angel asked when Lester and the children picked her up from work.

"Moses almost died," the children all chimed, almost bragging about his near-death experience. Lester tried to shush them, but it was to no avail when Angel saw the bloody scratches and bruises all over Moses's face.

"I know I'm not going to hear the end of this one," Lester said as he looked straight ahead while driving home.

Lester was Joy's hero. She told all her friends about Moses's accident and her father's bold response. Her friends would try to compete with Joy's stories, but couldn't come close. Joy and Moses followed Lester around the house like he was a celebrity. He could barely take a step without bumping into one of them because they were always close by. Joy felt safe when Lester was around. To her he was the greatest, and he would never let them down.

He was their savior.

CHAPTER FOUR

"Let the church say, 'Amen,'" Lester repeated, inhaling deeply like he was taking his last breath.

"Amen," Angel yelled as she stood to her feet, cheering Lester on as he concluded his initial sermon.

Though there were many Amens in the audience, Lester only heard Angel's. Not just because she was shouting at the top her lungs, but because her Amen was the only one that really mattered to him. Angel being proud of him was Lester's biggest motivation and her praise was what often compelled him to push himself, even when he didn't feel like moving forward.

As Lester stared into the audience, he thought about the call to ministry two years prior. It was a calling he could not ignore. When he recognized God was speaking to him, he decided to listen. He discussed his desire to go to seminary school with Angel and they agreed Howard School of Divinity was a good choice. On this night in 1985, Lester preached his initial sermon in the same church where he and Angel married eight years earlier, but this time Lester was poised in the pulpit, wearing a long black robe with a gold cross stitched on each side of the front panel.

Lester continued to survey the crowd and noticed Moses and Joy sprawled out on the hard wooden pew, one on each side of Angel. He didn't know if that was a bad sign that his own children fell asleep during his initial sermon, but he didn't take it personally. He imagined Angel trying to keep them awake was too draining for her, especially with all the standing up, sitting down, shouting, and clapping she'd been doing for the last hour.

After service, Lester shook everyone's hand who came to greet him. Joy and Moses woke up just in time to shake Lester's hand after service and tell him how great he was. Lester told them he heard them snoring during the sermon, so next time they would have to sit in the front row.

Lester gathered the family and drove home feeling drained physically, but on a spiritual and emotional high. He couldn't believe all the blessings he'd received since he married Angel. He was almost expecting something horrible to happen because he'd never felt this good. He was respected by his family, church, and community. He had so much to be thankful for, but braced himself for the battles that lay ahead. He tried not to think about what was next, but live in the amazing moment he had just experienced. He couldn't believe he was an ordained minister, and his family and friends couldn't believe it either. Nobody thought this smooth-talking guy from the streets could be a minister. A man who once used his wide smile and slick words to get close to the ladies now desired to win souls for Christ.

When they arrived at home, the kids were asleep in the backseat while Angel was fighting to stay awake and make small talk with Lester. Lester carried Joy and Moses inside and put them to bed. When he climbed into bed, Angel was already asleep. Lester said his prayers and kissed Angel on the forehead.

"I know I don't deserve this, but Lord, I thank you."

· · · · ·

Saturday afternoon Lester and Joy went to Lexington Market in downtown Baltimore to get a chicken box, cheese-steak sub, and a few items for Angel. They strolled through the market a while, collecting the things on their list as they took in the sights and sounds of the busy place.

"Hey, Coconut. What's up, man? How ya been?" Lester asked.

"Hey, Les, what's happening? Where you been hiding?"

"Just living, doing the family thing. This is my daughter, Joy. Isn't she gorgeous?"

"Yeah, man, she is going to be a heartbreaker. You better watch out for them knuckle-head boys."

"Yeah, I know. You know I'm a minister now. "

"A what?" Coconut laughed hysterically. "Stop, man, you're killing me. Stop playing. You, a minister—get real."

"I'm as serious as a heart attack. I'm a minister. What's so funny about that? People change, you know. I'm not the same person you grew up with. I'm a better man."

"Oh, I'm sorry, Les, I didn't mean nothing by it. You just caught me off guard with the religious talk. That's good, congratulations."

"Thanks, man, it was good seeing you. Take care, keep the faith."

"You, too, Les. Later."

Lester grabbed Joy's hand and they continued to stroll through the market.

"Dad, where do you know him from?"

"He's an old friend of mine."

"Why was he surprised that you're a minister?"

"Well some people expect you to stay the same. When we hung out, church was the farthest thing from our minds. So that shocked him, I guess."

"Oh. You should have invited him to church, so he could hear you preach."

"That's a good idea. The next time I bump into him I'll do that. That's why you make me so proud, 'cause you're so smart. You bring tears of joy to my eyes." Lester covered his face with his hand and pretended like he was wiping tears from his eyes.

"Daddy, stop joking around."

Even though Joy acted like Lester annoyed her, he knew she loved spending time with him.

Lester and Joy headed home once they gathered all the items on their list. With a few extra food stops and Lester giving Joy one of many historic lessons on the city of Baltimore, it was getting late and the family had to prepare for church the next day.

Lester wanted Joy and Moses to have a healthy childhood, and he thought if they spent most of their time in church they were destined to turn out great. On Sundays they rose early and ate breakfast as a family before heading to Sunday School, followed by worship service. Morning service ended around two-thirty, then they returned for evening service at five o'clock. Between morning and evening service, Angel prepared an elaborate meal and invited some of the church members over for dinner. When evening service concluded after seven-thirty, it was close to Moses and Joy's bedtime.

Since Lester was an associate minister, it was only right that the rest of the family became involved. Angel became a Sunday School teacher, taught Vacation Bible School, and sang in the Women's Day choir, while Joy and Moses joined the youth choir and the youth usher board. In addition to spending their Sundays in church, they were there practically every day of the week.

· · · · ·

A year after Lester was ordained, his father became ill. He was the only grandfather Joy and Moses ever knew. They didn't see him often and Lester rarely mentioned him. However, when Lester's father, Clifford, became ill, they started visiting him on a regular basis.

Clifford was dark-skinned, short, overweight, and had white hair that looked silver in the light. He coughed a lot, the kind of cough that made your throat hurt when you heard it because it sounded so bad. The children told Lester they didn't like visiting him because his house smelled like urine and he wasn't nice.

Clifford, a recovering alcoholic, was never really a part of Lester's life. Lester told Joy about a Christmas when his father stopped by with a huge duffel bag filled with gifts for him and his siblings. He explained how excited he and his siblings were when they saw the gifts. Their eyes lit up and they started jumping up and down. When they asked their father what he brought them, he explained the gifts were for his girlfriend's kids. Lester said his sister Reese cried the whole night after their father left. He started tearing up at the end of that story.

"I never want to be like my father. I want you, your mother, and Moses to always be proud of me," Lester said as he hugged Joy tightly.

After Lester shared that memory with Joy, he realized most of the pain of his past was still a problem for him. He never confronted Clifford about not being there for him, but he knew it was necessary and feared if he waited any longer it would be too late. Lester decided to visit Clifford one afternoon alone for a talk.

"Hey, old man. How you feeling?" Lester asked, trying to make small talk.

"I've been better, son." Clifford coughed like it pained him to speak.

"You know I don't know when the right time is to have this conversation, but I wanted to talk to you about our relationship."

"What about it?" Clifford sighed.

Lester stood over Clifford lying in bed, knowing this conversation would be a waste of time, but he couldn't leave until he got this off his chest.

"Well, we didn't have one. You were never there for me or any of my brothers and sisters growing up. I want to know why." Lester rubbed his hands from his forehead to the nape of his neck several times while he waited for a response.

"Why? What?" Clifford appeared irritated by the conversation and shifted his body away from Lester and folded his arms.

Lester walked around his bed so he could see Clifford's face when he asked the question he'd held in for his entire life. "Why weren't you there for any of your children? Why weren't you there for me?" Lester knelt by his bedside, positioning his face so close to Clifford's his nostrils burned from the smell of alcohol on his breath.

Clifford shrugged his shoulders, hoping Lester would leave him alone. "I don't know."

"I'm not leaving until you give me an answer." Lester

reliving all the memories of his childhood without having his father around made him weep like the day he was shipped off to foster care.

"I didn't know how to be there." Clifford sat up and leaned his back against the wooden headboard to support him as he cleared his throat. Reaching for a napkin to release the mucous in his mouth, he spoke again after what seemed to be an eternity for Lester. "My father was never there for me. In fact, I didn't know who he was and I never cared to find him."

Lester was still kneeling by his bedside, clinging to every word, searching for something that would help him move past the pain he'd carried all this time.

"I didn't look forward to being a father. I just happened to have kids. Though I have a lot of kids of which I am proud, I don't know how to be a father to any of you. In my old age I feel it's too late to start. I apologize for not being there, but I couldn't be what I never had." Clifford stared at the ceiling, avoiding eye contact with Lester at all cost.

"Look at me. The very least you can do is look at me." Lester stood and wiped his face with a handkerchief he pulled from his back pocket. "That's just an excuse because I am the father I never had. You just didn't want to try." Lester stood over Clifford, ready to walk out the house and release the burden he'd been carrying for so long, but before leaving he leaned down and hugged him.

"I love you, Dad, and I forgive you. I pray you can forgive yourself."

Clifford broke down and cried on Lester's shoulder. He tried to hold his emotions in, but as he stared death in the face, he had more bad days than good and he knew what he'd done to his children would follow him to his grave.

Several weeks after Lester's last visit, Clifford died. His funeral was sterile and the program was succinct. Joy sat between Lester and Angel with Moses on the end. Lester cried like a baby at the funeral.

"Everything is going to be all right, Dad." Joy held onto his arm and leaned her head on his shoulder. Joy had never seen Lester so upset.

Lester's siblings shed a few tears, but none of them wept like him except for his baby sister, Jillian. He noticed that one of his sisters didn't cry at all. He later told Angel that he didn't understand how someone could be so cold toward her own father.

The funeral was on a Saturday night. The next morning before church, Joy and Moses hopped on Lester and Angel's bed.

Lester could tell when Joy was bursting with a question for him. He assumed it had something to do with his father's funeral.

"Is something on your mind, Joy?" Lester asked before Joy exploded.

"Where do people go when they die?" Joy asked, amazed that Lester always knew when something was on her mind.

"Well, if they are saved, meaning if they accept Jesus into their heart, they go to Heaven. But if they don't do that, then they go to hell," Lester responded.

"What is Heaven like?" Joy asked.

"Heaven is a beautiful place where Jesus lives and there is no pain. The streets are paved in gold and the gates are made of pearls. Hell is a place where people burn and suffer forever."

"I want to go to Heaven, Dad. How do I get saved?" Joy asked like her life depended on his answer.

"You need to believe that Jesus is Lord, he died for the sins of the world, and was raised from the dead. Then you need to repeat the prayer of salvation. Do you believe Jesus died for your sins?"

"Yes," Joy and Moses chimed in.

"Then repeat after me. Dear God, I know that You love me. I confess my sins and need of salvation. I believe Jesus died on the cross for my sins and arose from the grave. I turn away from my sins and place my faith in Jesus as my Savior and Lord. I want to follow You with my life. Amen."

Joy and Moses got down on their knees and repeated the prayer of salvation. They asked Jesus Christ to come into their hearts and received the gift of salvation. Before they were conceived, this moment was pre-ordained by God. Who better to lead them to Christ than their father, the man they respected and loved?

Later that morning in church they made their decision public and walked down the center aisle when the invitation to Christ was given at the end of service. Everyone in the church rejoiced. That was the winter of 1986, a day Moses and Joy would remember for eternity.

CHAPTER FIVE

All the time Lester spent working in ministry caused a strain on Lester and Angel's relationship. Angel tried to help Lester prepare for sermons and bring the kids to all of his preaching assignments, but she couldn't work full-time, care for their children, and be there for her husband at all times. When Lester started preaching Angel was always in the second pew, shouting the loudest, but as time passed she started slipping to the back of the church to catch the end of a sermon when he preached during the week, and sometimes she couldn't make them at all.

Lester and Angel evangelized on Saturdays in Baltimore City with Moses and Joy by their side as they knocked on doors, spreading the good news. People admired their dedication to Christ and the testimony of a family who served God together.

Angel prayed for God to sustain her as a wife and mother, because she knew it would take His supernatural power to be all things to her family. As Lester's schedule became more demanding as a minister, he began to neglect his full-time job. In fact, Angel found out he'd been fired for weeks before he told her what had happened. With Lester being quick-witted and eloquent, he was never unemployed for a very long time.

"You know I'm preaching Easter Sunday at the church, so I want everybody to be ready on time," Lester reminded Angel as she dressed for work on Good Friday.

"I know, sweetie. We'll be ready. I already picked up Joy's Easter outfit and I will take Moses to the mall, so I can get him a suit." Angel smiled as she rubbed Lester's shoulders.

"Good, this is going to be an important Sunday. You know most people who don't attend church will visit only twice a year, Easter and Christmas. So this is a great opportunity to win souls for Christ and compel unbelievers to accept Him."

"Amen. I'm so proud of you, honey. That was so nice of Pastor Davis to let you preach on Easter Sunday. He normally preaches himself. Did you finish your sermon notes?"

"Almost. I'll work on that today."

"Aren't you supposed to go to work today?" Angel asked as she tilted her head.

"I took the day off to prepare for the sermon." Lester abruptly moved Angel's hands from his shoulders and walked out of their bedroom.

Angel stretched across the bed and prayed this was not the beginning of Lester losing another job. The scenario was always the same. He would start to take a few days off to prepare for a sermon or attend a church-related function, and then his supervisor would give him a permanent vacation.

Angel wanted to move into their own home desperately, but she worried Lester's reckless behavior would be too much to bear if they moved out of her mother's house.

Gran never said anything to Lester or Angel about Lester's work habits. A marriage was hard enough for a couple without the meddling of a mother-in-law, but Angel knew she too was concerned that Lester would not be able to provide a stable home for Angel and the kids.

Over the weekend Angel ran herself ragged, running from store to store to find a suit for Moses and patent leather shoes for Joy. She always wanted them to look picture-perfect for Resurrection Sunday service.

It was tradition on the Saturday before to dye Easter eggs for baskets and the family Easter egg hunt after dinner. Easter dinner was always at Gran's house. Gran and Angel stayed up half the night, preparing an elaborate meal. Early the next morning they rose to finish cooking and decorate the house.

When Angel finished cooking she woke the children up and got them ready for service. This was one of those days when Angel operated on prayer and pure adrenaline to get her through the day. Before the Noble family left for church, they took pictures to savor the moment. Joy dressed in a purple and white dress, white straw hat, and white patent leather shoes, while Moses was dressed in a navy blue suit with a white shirt and purple tie.

They kissed Gran goodbye and piled into the family car, headed for church. Angel sang along to the gospel radio station as they traveled. When they pulled into the church parking lot it was packed. In fact, there was a line outside the door. Lester's sermon, "He's Alive," brought Angel to tears. As she listened to all that Christ suffered for every person, she was reminded of how much He loved her. She thought about His mercy and His goodness and couldn't help but jump to her feet and give Him praise.

When Angel jumped up and said, "Hallelujah," Moses and Joy jumped up and shouted, "Hallelujah," too. It took Angel a few moments to notice them jumping and waving their hands.

"You two better not be playing with the Lord. I will not tolerate you mocking God." Angel leaned down to Joy and Moses and gave them the don't-make-me-jack-you-up-in-church look.

"We're not playing, Mom. We want to praise God, too," Joy proclaimed while Moses nodded in agreement.

Angel was surprised by their response but confident they were being honest. She smiled and gave them the nod of approval to carry on. They'd been in church all their lives, so it was only a matter of time before they stopped playing in church and decided to participate in praising God.

At the end of service, Angel and the children waited for Lester to greet and shake everyone's hand. When they arrived at Gran's, Angel's extended family was already there ready for dinner.

All of the cousins rushed to change out of their Easter outfits and into their play clothes. After dinner the kids started the Easter egg hunt while the adults ate dessert, drank coffee, and caught up on each other's busy lives.

Everyone was enjoying themselves when they heard someone screaming and a loud rolling down the steep stairs to the basement, followed by a hard thud at the bottom of the steps. Angel ran to the top of the stairs to see what had happened. When she looked down, there was Moses crying at the bottom of the steps, surrounded by Joy and all their cousins.

"Lester, Moses fell down the steps," Angel yelled as she frantically ran down the stairs.

Somehow Lester managed to beat her to the bottom. Moses was crying, as he was in excruciating pain and couldn't move. While standing next to Lester as he examined him, Angel noticed his left leg swelled to the point of ripping his jeans, and his left foot almost burst out of his sneaker. Lester bolted upstairs, grabbed a pair of scissors from the kitchen cabinet, then returned to Moses's side in seconds. He cut up the seam of Moses's pants and took off his tennis shoe to help his circulation. Within a few moments, Moses's leg and foot swelled to an abnormal size.

Lester and Angel rushed Moses to the hospital. Angel told Joy to stay at home with the rest of the family until they returned. The three waited in the emergency room for an hour before Moses was helped. The doctor said he had never seen a case like this and recommended they consult a children's oncologist because the X-rays showed a mass in Moses's leg. The doctor was not sure what it was, but knew an oncologist could give them more information. He also recommended icing his leg to reduce some of the swelling.

"Dad, what's an oncologist?" Moses asked as he leaned on Lester's chest.

"A special doctor, that's all. You'll be fine. Don't worry. What do I always tell you when you're afraid?"

"Where faith resides, fear cannot," Moses said with confidence.

Shortly after they got in the car, Moses fell asleep in the backseat and Angel started weeping silently.

"Why are you crying?" Lester whispered.

"What if the mass is cancerous?"

"The power of life and death lies in the tongue. You know that. So why are you claiming cancer?"

"I'm not claiming anything, but Moses has a mass in his leg and we've been recommended to a child oncologist." Angel cried into her handkerchief.

"Woman, where is your faith?"

"How dare you question my faith," Angel snapped.

"The devil is a liar. We serve a God of power. In the name of Jesus I pray Moses is healed. He does not have cancer."

They rode the rest of the way in silence. When they arrived at home, the entire family was waiting to hear the diagnosis. Lester told everyone they had to see a specialist on Monday and they asked everyone to pray.

They didn't share the details with anyone except Gran after Joy and Moses went to bed.

Later that night, Lester knelt at the foot of Moses's bed and prayed for hours.

The next morning Lester called family and friends and asked them to pray for Moses at 10 a.m., when he saw the specialist. After Lester made his phone calls he gathered the family together for prayer. Lester and Angel decided to fast until after Moses's appointment. They only wanted to focus on God and His healing power.

Gran waved goodbye as everyone piled into the family car. "I know everything is going to be okay."

Lester and Angel dropped Joy off at school on the way to the hospital.

"Why can't I go to the hospital with everyone else?" Joy folded her arms as she got out of the car.

"Because you should be in school learning," Angel said while she motioned Joy over to the car window and kissed her on the cheek. "Love you. We'll pick you up from school."

Joy walked slowly up the hill to the auditorium. While they waited for Joy to make it up the hill, she turned around and walked back to the car.

"I was wondering if you changed your mind and decided to let me go to the hospital," Joy said with the saddest look she could invoke.

"Joy, we know you want to be there for Moses, but it's best you go to school. Everything is going to be fine. We'll all come to pick you up this afternoon. Okay?" Angel hugged Joy through the car window. "Now hurry up the hill so we can make it to the hospital on time."

In the car ride on the way to the hospital, gospel music played softly in the background while Lester and Angel made small talk with Moses. They weren't going to focus on his foot and leg because they didn't want him to worry, but since Moses's swelling went down completely they focused on that to make him feel at ease.

"How do you feel, Moses?" Angel turned around from the front seat to see Moses's little face while she spoke with him.

"I feel fine, Mom."

"Good. Everything is going to be fine. We have the entire world praying for you. God hears our prayers. Do you believe that?" Angel smiled as she turned and looked at Lester to gauge how he was really handling everything.

"Ah, Mom."

"Yes, Mo."

"If they find something wrong with my foot or my leg, what will happen?"

There was an awkward moment of silence before Angel responded. She hoped this would be one of the moments Lester interjected, but he had been quiet for most of the car ride.

"I'm not sure. The specialist will give us more information after he examines you. Don't worry about something being wrong."

"Moses, name one thing you know about Jesus," Lester said as he looked at Moses squirm in the rearview mirror.

Angel felt for Moses because he despised being put on the spot. She didn't know why Lester was drilling him at a time like this.

"That He is God the son," Moses replied.

"Yes, He is God the son, but what about some of the things He did?"

"He performed miracles."

"Yes. Do you remember any of the miracles He performed?"

"Ahh, He made a blind man see."

"Exactly! He has all power. There is nothing He can't do. He made the blind man see. He performed many other miracles, but do you know what was key about the blind man who was healed? He believed he could be healed. So did the lame man who Jesus told to pick up his mat and walk. They had the faith that they would be healed. Moses, do you believe Jesus heals today?"

"Yes."

"So that means if you believe, even if something was wrong with you, Jesus can heal you. No matter what happens, I want you to believe that and know nothing can happen to you unless God allows it."

"I know, Dad."

Moses walked between Lester and Angel, holding their hands as they strolled to the hospital entrance. They took the elevator up three flights. When the silver elevator doors opened to the fourth floor, they were amazed to see most of their family members waiting for them. Gran rushed to the elevator to hug Moses and cheer him up.

"We couldn't let you three come to the hospital alone. We're a family, and family that prays together stays together," Gran said as she tussled Moses's curly brown hair while he held onto her waist.

"We're glad you all showed up. I should have known Gran had something up her sleeve when she rushed us out this morning," Lester said as he held Angel's hand. "I want to thank all of you for your prayers and for your presence now. Speaking of prayer, I would like us to get in a circle with Moses standing in the middle and pray. On the drive here, I asked Moses if he believed Jesus could heal. In the Bible it tells us that Jesus has all power and that as His believers, not only can we do the things He did, but we can do greater things in Jesus's name. So that means on this morning we can all witness a miracle. When we took Moses to the emergency room yesterday, the doctor took X-rays of his leg and foot and said there was a mass. He told us to see this child oncologist right away, but I serve a God who heals and I speak in the name of Jesus my son is healed. Whatever the doctor saw is gone in the name of Jesus. There is power in the name of Jesus. Let us pray."

As they prayed in the circle, the medical staff stopped and bowed their heads out of respect for the family. When they said "Amen," Dr. Lawrence spoke with Lester and Angel.

"Hi, I'm Doctor Lawrence. You must be the Noble family. I wasn't expecting thirty people to show up for this appointment." He smiled as he reviewed the notes on his clipboard.

"We didn't expect it either, Doctor Lawrence. I'm Lester Noble and this is my wife, Angel, and this is Moses."

"Good to meet you. We're going to run several tests on Moses and ask him a series of questions about his fall and the pain he felt and how he feels right now. We have several labs on site, so we will have the results in a few hours. Mr. Noble, you and your wife can come back with Moses for the questions, and then we will ask you to return to the waiting room while we run the tests."

They ran tests for almost two hours. A series of blood tests and MRI scans. Now the family had to wait for the results. Lester prayed and read his Bible most of the morning. That calmed him when everyone else was anxious. That also distracted him from his grumbling stomach, as he hadn't eaten since Moses fell.

"Mr. and Mrs. Noble, we have the test results. Would you like to discuss them privately?" Dr. Lawrence appeared to suppress a smile.

Lester stood tall with his arms crossed. "You can tell us here in front of our family." "Well, we've looked at the test results and examined and re-examined the X-rays every possible way and we don't see anything. I can't explain what the other doctor saw, or thought he saw yesterday, and I don't know why Moses's foot and leg swelled yesterday, because there is not as much as a sprain on any part of his foot or leg. The results show Moses is healthy and everything is normal."

Cheers of "Amen," "Hallelujah," and "Thank you, Jesus" broke out in the waiting room. A miracle happened right before their eyes. Moses leapt for joy, and this shy boy danced like nobody had ever seen.

"Thank you, Jesus, for healing me," Moses shouted as he hugged Lester tightly around his neck.

"God is good, Dad. I love you."

"Yes, He is, son. I love you, too. Let's go pick up your sister and tell her the good news."

CHAPTER SIX

"Thank you, God, for hearing and answering our prayers. Lord, I praise You for healing my baby. You are worthy, Jesus. You are worthy of all praise and glory. Thank you, Lord. Hallelujah to Your name, Jesus." Angel prayed out loud as she stood at the altar of the church embracing Lester with one arm clutched tightly at the bottom of his back, while her other arm held Moses and Joy to her side.

At Sunday morning service a week after Moses's fall, the pastor asked the Nobles to come forward and share the miracle of Moses's healing. After Moses testified about his leg, Angel worshipped God with the words she uttered and wept as she thought about His faithfulness to her family. Angel held her family close and prayed silently that nothing would ever separate their bond.

Angel returned to the rhythm of life as a career woman, wife, and mother, but she did not return the same. She got up earlier in the morning and knelt by Lester's side of the bed and prayed for him and their marriage. Then she walked the narrow hallway to the children's room and knelt in the middle of the floor and prayed for Joy and Moses. Rising from the floor, she always stopped in Gran's room last, and Gran was always waiting by her bed with a Bible. There the two read scripture and prayed for their family. Angel couldn't let go of the supernatural high she experienced and the rush she felt when the doctors could no longer find the mass in Moses's leg. She replayed the fall, the emergency room visit, and that joyous day when the doctor gave them the good news.

She watched her family get better. They were more passionate about life and concerned for one another's well-being. Angel was grateful she didn't have to break up fights between Moses and Joy on a daily basis like the days before the fall.

Angel found herself boisterously singing praises to God and telling everyone she knew how blessed she was to have her family. Before Moses's accident, she felt like the tightly woven family was beginning to unravel. It was still one beautiful piece of embroidery, but there was a string that was waiting to be pulled and slowly undo the years of sweat put into every stitch. It was like God put this moment in their lives to appreciate each other and focus on all they had instead of what would happen next. Angel was convicted about her late hours at work and vowed to wrap up earlier, so she could make Lester and the kids the priority.

Since Lester got a new job he wasn't at home as much with the children, and Angel felt she should pick up the slack and not leave the children alone so much with Gran, though she knew she didn't mind. Angel rejoiced when Lester announced he got a new job where he managed a community outreach for male adolescents. Lester repeatedly described every detail of how he designed social programs to increase the number of high school graduates from disadvantaged homes in Baltimore City to Angel. He wouldn't come up for air as he described the young men he worked with at the community center. As his shoulders straightened and his chest puffed up like a proud peacock, his eyes beamed with pride. Angel saw how having a career Lester was passionate about made his life more meaningful. She knew their family meant a lot to him, but understood his vocation gave him an identity. She remained silent when he was unemployed because she knew he was ashamed he couldn't provide for his family. Angel was thankful Lester finally found a job where he was positioned for a purpose. It wasn't just about the money, but about the message of hope he could model for the males in the program. She could tell how much this job meant to Lester as he shared how he saw himself in the young men at the center.

Lester still preached some evenings and weekends, therefore his schedule was often hectic, but Angel was determined to maintain order in their home. Angel attended services with him when she could and encouraged Lester as she balanced the demands of being superwoman. She overlooked his late nights and retreats out of town as him doing the work of the Lord and providing for their family.

With Lester working they were getting closer to their savings goal to move out of Gran's house and into their own home. She felt blessed they could stay with Gran, because she watched the children when Angel and Lester were too busy and helped Angel with cooking and cleaning. However, with her sister Emma moving in, there was very little space, and they wanted Joy and Moses to get a better education. They couldn't afford private school much longer, so they desired a move to Baltimore County where the public school curriculum was equivalent to private schools in the city.

With their hectic schedules, Lester and Angel tried to keep Saturdays free for family outings. On one particularly crisp Saturday in October, they planned to go to the park and the cinema for a kid-friendly comedy.

While they were eating breakfast, there was a knock at the front door. Lester rose to get the door, but Gran insisted on getting it since she had already finished her meal. On her way to the front door, Gran straightened out the cloth on the dining room table that was slightly uneven. Angel followed Gran out of the kitchen and stopped in the dining room where she had a clear view of the door. She grabbed a cleaning rag to provide a decoy while she eavesdropped to see who was at the front door.

"Well, Pastor Davis, what a surprise to see you this morning." She patted her hair down and straightened her apron to make herself presentable for the senior pastor of her church. It was rare for the senior pastor to visit anyone's home without an invitation and without calling first.

"Good morning, Mother Sword. How are you?" asked the pastor as he kissed Gran on her cheek.

"Blessed and highly favored in the Lord." Gran waved her right hand as if she was going to testify to how good God had been to her.

"Well, praise the Lord. You are looking quite well. I would like to speak to Lester and Angel in private, if that's all right with you, of course."

"Sure, Pastor. They're eating breakfast with the kids. I'll get them for you. Have a seat."

Angel hurried back to the kitchen and waited for Gran to announce Pastor Davis.

"Angel and Lester, Pastor Davis is here to see you," Gran yelled as she walked to the back of the house. "I'll sit with the kids while they finish eating breakfast"

"I wonder what Pastor Davis wants." Angel leaned her head toward Lester.

"I have no idea," Lester said as he and Angel walked toward the living room.

"Good morning, Pastor. To what do we owe this pleasant surprise?" Angel asked as she hugged Pastor Davis.

"Good morning, Pastor." Lester shook his hand as they all sat down.

"Well, I'm not here for pleasantries, so I guess I'll cut to the chase. What I have to say is hard for me because I love you two like family, but as your pastor I have to maintain a standard in our church."

"What is this about?" Lester asked.

"Lester, a young woman stopped by the church last Saturday with her six-month-old son. She told me you fathered her child, and you refused to acknowledge your son or her. Her name is Sheila."

Lester leaned forward, and crossed his arms while he nervously tapped his right leg. His clenched jaw told Angel he was hiding something.

"The child is not mine," Lester proclaimed as a bead of sweat formed on his forehead.

"Is that all you have to say?" Angel leaned forward, almost falling out of her chair as she locked eyes with Lester, forcing him to look at her. She couldn't believe this was happening to her as the words poured out of Pastor Davis's mouth like kerosene on a flame that engulfed her heart. *How could he do this to me, to us?* Angel thought as she felt every inch of her body tie into knots of pain.

"I didn't come here to start a war in your home, but I had to address this situation directly because this will not be tolerated in our church. The little boy looks exactly like Moses and I don't think that is a coincidence."

"If you feed a child long enough it will look like you, so looks aren't really a solid indicator of genetics, Pastor," Lester said. "With all due respect, I don't appreciate this accusation."

How can he be so calm when he's being accused of something so horrible? It must be true, Angel thought as she bent over and placed her head on the pillow she'd put in her lap.

Adrenaline rushed from her forehead to her heels with every exchange between Lester and Pastor Davis.

"Do you know Sheila? Yes or no?"

"I know several Sheilas, sir."

"Okay, I see we are going to play games. Do you know a Sheila Matthews? Brown skin, shoulder-length hair, about thirty-five years old?"

"I do."

"Could you have fathered her child?"

There was an intense moment of silence where the only distraction was Lester's deep breathing and Angel's tears falling down her beautiful brown cheeks. Lester huffed and shrugged for several moments before he cleared his throat.

"It's possible."

"What?" Angel screamed as she jumped up, ready to lunge at Lester, but Pastor Davis stood up and firmly forced her flailing arms by her side and held her back so she couldn't grab Lester by the throat.

"How could you do this to me? I'm your wife, the mother of your children," Angel said over and over again until it became a whisper. Once she whispered it repeatedly, she screamed until the words bounced up to the ceiling and hit the floor with rage.

"Calm down, Angel. Have a seat and hear Lester out," Pastor Davis said as he helped her to the closest chair. "We don't want to alarm your mother and the kids."

"Explain!" Angel demanded as she leaned back in the antique chair with her eyes closed.

"I'm sorry." Lester reached for Angel's hand, but she snatched it away.

"I should have known all those late nights at church were nothing but a cover for your mess. You disgust me. We haven't been married for ten years and you're running around on me. No wonder you can't keep a job—you're too busy making babies."

"Angel, I'm sorry you found out this way," Pastor Davis said. "I'm going to leave, so you two can have your privacy. Lester, as the senior pastor, I am going to sit you down for one year. That means you will not preach at our church or any other church. You will not officiate weddings. You will not teach Bible study at our church or anywhere else, and you are required to come before the church and confess your sins. If you want to stay at the church, all of this is mandatory."

Lester stood up and responded to Pastor Davis's demands. "Wait a minute. Who are you to sit me down? Why do I have to confess to the church? The only person I have to confess to is God. What about the scripture in Matthew seven where it says, how can you say to your brother, 'Let me take the speck out of your eye,' when all the time there is a plank in your own eye?"

"I can't believe he has the gall to quote scripture. Help me, Lord. Please help me get out of this without losing my mind," Angel mumbled as she wiped the drops falling from her chin and nose.

Pastor Davis rose to stand eye to eye with Lester. He opened his pocket-sized Bible and flipped to a passage. "Brother Lester, I want you to remember what it says in Matthew eighteen, verses fifteen through seventeen. 'If your brother or sister sins, go and point out their fault, just between the two of you. If they listen to you, you have won them over. But if they will not listen, take one or two others along, so that every matter may be established by the testimony of two or three witnesses. If they still refuse to listen, tell it to the church; and if they refuse to listen even to the church, treat them as you would a pagan or a tax collector.' As the leader of Bibleway, it is my responsibility to keep order and peace in the church. I am not trying to embarrass you or point out your faults, because yes we all have faults. But I can't have a woman come to me with a child that looks exactly like you and tell me you fathered him, but that you will not acknowledge her or this child and act as if it didn't happen. As ministers we are supposed to set an example and that is what I am doing by sitting you down for one year."

Angel hunched over and cried. She couldn't believe how quickly her world had turned upside down. She wished this day had never happened.

"Pastor Davis, I've looked up to you as a father in ministry. I thank you for all you have been to me and my family, but I will not sit down or confess before the church. My family and I are leaving Bibleway and we will join another church." Lester extended his hand to Pastor Davis to shake it.

"I'm sorry to hear that, Lester. We consider you family. Your children were baptized at Bibleway. I married you and Angel. You don't deal with problems by running away, but as the man of your household I respect your decision and wish you and your family the best. I'm sorry about all of this, Angel." Pastor Davis exited the front door that Lester opened for him.

"Do you believe him? What nerve to tell me I have to sit down for a year." Lester shook his head in disgust.

Angel tried to keep herself from screaming at the top of her lungs to wake from what seemed to be a nightmare, but she knew Gran and the kids were still in the kitchen and she didn't want to alarm them.

"What should he have said?"

"Excuse me?" Lester's eyes widened.

"What should Pastor Davis have done and said, in your opinion?"

"Nothing. It is none of his business."

"I see. Well, it is my business as your wife." Angel wiped her face, then gripped the arms of the chair so she wouldn't stand and be tempted to squeeze the life out of Lester's thick neck. "I will not tolerate you cheating on me. So you decide what life you want to live. Do you want to be a husband, father, and minister? Or do you want to be a rolling stone? Let me know."

"Is that how you talk to your husband? With all we've been through, you just disrespect me because of a mistake I made?"

"So you accidentally met up with a woman and slept with her and fathered her child? A mistake is hardly the word for the mess you've created. What about this poor child? Are you going to see him? Start paying child support? Maybe we should pray about taking him in and raising him with Joy and Moses."

"Woman, are you crazy? The child is not mine."

"According to Pastor Davis, the child looks just like you!"

"What does that mean? That does not prove a thing. I am sorry for putting you through this." Lester kneeled by Angel's chair and grabbed her hand, but she snatched it away and turned her face to the window. "I love you and the children."

Angel shook her head from side to side. She turned from the window and looked at Lester. She grabbed her chest to calm the beating of her heart, and declared, "I don't think you know what love is, and that explains how you could betray me and break the covenant you made with God to love me like Christ loved the church."

"You've shown me how to love. The children opened my eyes to love. You know family means everything to me. There is no place else I want to be. Please forgive me," Lester begged as he stayed on his knees beside Angel and looked at her with those piercing eyes that always convinced her to believe whatever he said.

"Not this time, Les. You have crossed the line and ruined our relationship."

"What did Paul say? When I want to do good, evil is right there with me."

"You have the nerve to quote the Bible. Who did I marry? So much power and you can't keep your pants on?"

"I've had enough. I apologized and I don't want to discuss this any more. As a Christian the only thing you are supposed to do is forgive me. I'm going out for some air. Tomorrow we will start looking for a new church." Lester jumped up and slammed the door behind him.

Angel fell to her knees, buried her face in the worn seat cushion, and wept. She cried until the tears dried and there was nothing left inside her tired body to release. Her eyes were red and puffy from the rough wad of Kleenex she used to wipe her face. She didn't want to be in a marriage where there was no trust, but she didn't want her family split in two. Angel never thought Lester would cheat on her. She put so much effort into making him happy. How could Lester be so selfish? She cringed when she thought about the life he created with some other woman and felt faint at the notion of explaining this child to Joy and Moses.

"Lord, please give me the strength to forgive Lester for what he's done. Help me move on in peace, so our family won't be broken. I pray if this child is Lester's, you will make it known and give this little boy a place in our hearts and home."

"In Jesus' name. Amen," Gran said softly as she hugged her tightly from behind.

CHAPTER SEVEN

"Dad, why are we visiting all these churches? We miss Bibleway. That's where all my friends are and we haven't been there in weeks. My friends are saying we don't go to the church anymore," Joy stated as she leaned as close as she could to the driver's seat without unfastening her seatbelt.

Angel hummed "Amazing Grace" as it played on the radio while she stared at Lester, awaiting his response.

"We are visiting new churches because we've been at Bibleway for a while, and I think we've outgrown that church. I want us to continue to be challenged by the word. I want us to be in a larger church where there is more opportunity for ministry. Therefore, we won't be going back to Bibleway."

"I don't want to join another church. What about my friends?" Joy leaned back and rolled her eyes. She didn't understand why adults changed things that weren't messed up in the first place.

"Joy, that's enough. I don't need your input on where we go to church. You're a child. I make the decisions for this family," Lester said as he kept his eyes on the road, while he tightly gripped the steering wheel.

They were on their way to Mount Holiness Baptist Church, located between a small abandoned convenience store and row houses. The brick-front narrow houses were connected on both sides and the only thing that separated the red bricks on this particular block was the tiny white church on the corner.

What kind of run-down, make-shift church are we visiting? Joy thought as they parked.

Joy sighed and rolled her eyes as she unfastened her seatbelt. Then she nudged Moses and pointed to the church building while shaking her head in disgust as if this experience was the worst thing that could happen to them.

When they arrived at the front door, the pastor's mother, wife, and son greeted the Noble family and Gran. Those three, plus the pastor and ten other people, completed the congregation that morning.

Gran accompanied them to service because she knew the pastor. The head usher, who was the pastor's mother and the resident nurse, led Angel, Gran, Moses, and Joy to their seats like there was a crowd waiting. She wore a crisp white uniform. The dress came to the top of her calf and left her bony legs swimming in an opaque pair of white stockings, like a goldfish in a large aquarium. The church mother had on a pair of white gloves and a nametag that read *Head Usher*. It took her about five minutes to guide them six pews to the front and seat them.

Joy noticed an aroma of damp clothes and fried chicken filled the sanctuary as she tried to get comfortable. The wooden pews weren't covered with cushions like Bibleway. The hard pews meant one thing for Joy: she wouldn't take a nap during service.

Lester was seated in the pulpit next to the pastor and the pastor's wife, while the rest of the family was seated in the second pew from the front of the church. The church was so small; if Joy had a pointing stick, she could have touched the platform of the pulpit.

The pastor welcomed everyone to service and opened with a prayer, then asked the choir to render a selection. The choir was comprised of the pastor's wife, his son, and mother. They rose with the fanfare of a large mass choir, syncing their steps to the microphones, coordinating their hand claps, and swaying like they were opening for the Temptations. At least their theatrics distracted from the tone-deaf rendition of "Going Up Yonder." When the choir finished singing, the pastor introduced the guest preacher, the right Reverend Noble.

Is he preaching about forgiveness again? Joy rolled her eyes and folded her arms in boredom.

At the end of the sermon the pastor asked everyone to stand and sing a verse of "Blessed Assurance," then he gave the invitation to salvation, where anyone who had never confessed Jesus Christ as Lord and Savior could walk forward and do so in front of the congregation. When no one came forward to receive Christ or join the church, the pastor stepped down from the pulpit and randomly picked people out of the congregation to come forward.

"I feel like Satan is in this building today. Some of you are hurting and scared. You need to confess your sins. Come forward, Satan. Come out, demons," the Pastor declared as he paced back and forth at the front of the church, staring into the audience.

Joy was thinking about Bibleway and yearned to be there. She started blinking uncontrollably, wiping the tear drops, so Moses wouldn't make fun of her crying. When the Pastor saw Joy's tears, he walked to her row, grabbed her by the arm, and pulled her to the front of the church. Joy tried to go back to her seat, but that pastor's grip got tighter. The pastor put some oil on her forehead and laid his hands on her skull.

"Satan, come out of this child. I know you have a hold on this child. Let her loose, Satan. I command the demons to leave this vessel."

Gran walked to the front of the church and stood next to Joy and rubbed her back. The pastor put his hands on Joy's head and pressed his hands on the front and back of her skull so hard, Joy felt like she was going to fall over from the pressure. It was like Joy's head was a lemon and the pastor wanted lemonade.

What am I going to do? This man is crazy, Joy thought. With her eyes closed tightly she prayed silently while the pastor continued to perform. *Lord, please show me a way out. Please give me a sign.*

When Joy opened her eyes the sun was shining through the windows by the entrance, so she bolted out the door, leaving the pastor and congregation in a cloud of dust.

Joy stood outside by the family car and waited for everyone to exit. Since her parents were the only way home, she hoped they weren't going to stay for the chicken dinner. She could tell church was over because the congregation, all ten of them, trickled out. The pastor walked Lester, Angel, Gran, and Moses out. Joy wanted to hide, but there was no escape. She didn't want the pastor to finish what he thought he started.

"Please don't be alarmed." The pastor smiled as he slowly approached Joy with his hand extended toward her. "I apologize for startling you," the pastor said as he shook Joy's hand gently. Joy quickly pulled her hand back and stared at the man she thought was so strange.

"When I looked into the congregation, I saw your tears and in my spirit I felt like you were wrestling with demons. Lester told me you're upset because you miss your old church. Please accept my apology, I didn't mean to frighten you. I'm sorry about this, Reverend Noble and family. I hope you'll stop by and visit us again soon."

Joy exhaled in relief when he finally concluded his farewells and vanished into the church.

"Sorry I ran out, Mom and Dad, but I didn't know what else to do," Joy said.

"We're not mad, Joy. I was completely caught off guard and I know he startled you," Angel said as she hugged Joy.

Gran hugged her and stroked her hair. "Are you okay? I wanted to rescue you, but I couldn't. I don't know why that fool did that to you."

"Mom," Angel exclaimed at Gran's use of words.

"Well, he is a fool. Why else would he do something like that to a child?" Gran looked up at the sky. "Lord, please forgive me for calling the pastor a fool, at least in front of the children."

When they got in the car, everyone burst into laughter. Joy could laugh now that she was safe in the car and not in the preacher's death grip. This was one of the many church adventures for the Nobles. Every Sunday Joy didn't know what to expect. If it wasn't a preacher laying forceful hands on her, it was showing up to a church that was boarded up, or having service in someone's living room while the family dog ran through the make-shift sanctuary. Joy didn't want to visit any more churches; she wanted to return to Bibleway.

A few weeks after the church visit from hell, they attended several more churches. Finally, they joined Plymouth Baptist Church in Baltimore County where Angel's sister, Diane, and her two sons were members. Joy was tired of bouncing from church to church, and knew Moses and Angel were sick of it, too, but no one would dare confront Lester.

Diane's church had a white pastor and a diverse congregation, which was a change for the Nobles. The building was much larger than Bibleway, with several hundred more people in the congregation.

Lester became an associate minister about a year after they joined Plymouth Baptist. The pastor, Reverend Joel Wright, was sound in doctrine and Joy liked listening to him. He preached about sin and how the devil tries to tempt God's children. He was interesting, too. She found the way he explained the Bible intriguing. It was almost like he was an actor. While his tall, thin frame stood in the pulpit, he took the scripture and explained it simply so anyone could apply it to real life. Sometimes Reverend Wright stepped down from the pulpit and walked into the congregation while he expounded on his preaching points. His blond hair would flop from side to side when he jumped around and went in for the dramatic conclusion to his sermon.

The members were friendly and embraced the Nobles. They welcomed them into their homes for Sunday dinners and helped them easily transition into being active members of Plymouth. There were a lot of kids, which was a bonus for Moses and Joy. They began to make friends, and though they missed their buddies from Bibleway, it made their new church a lot of fun. Joy could tell Lester was thrilled to have a position at a church again because he spent a lot of time at Plymouth.

Joy was surprised they joined a congregation with a white pastor because Lester talked about the black man being oppressed every opportunity he got, but he had to curtail his racial commentary when he preached at Plymouth or say goodbye to being an associate minister.

A few months after becoming members of Plymouth, Joy wondered why they left Bibleway. She tried to remember the last service she attended there to see if something out of the ordinary took place, but she couldn't think of anything. She thought her family, especially Lester, loved the church. When Joy bumped into one of her friends from Bibleway, she mentioned that her parents told her Lester had gotten into a fight with Pastor Davis and that was why they left.

Joy just knew her friend heard wrong, because Pastor Davis and Lester were close friends. Whenever Joy asked Lester about leaving Bibleway, he would give the same response about it being necessary to grow. When she asked Angel, she would always defer to Lester with an annoyed look.

Joy decided to be content with finally having found a good church where she made friends, and the pew cushions were soft.

CHAPTER EIGHT

"Okay, you can take off your blindfolds," Angel shouted gleefully. "It's our new home."

"Wow," Moses and Joy said in unison as they jumped out of the car and ran up the steps.

Before Angel could unlock the door, Joy and Moses argued over who would get the second largest bedroom in the house.

Within six months of joining Plymouth, the Nobles moved into a single-family house in Baltimore County. Their home was five minutes from Plymouth, which made their commute to church convenient. Angel was so excited when moving day arrived, she and Lester blindfolded the kids and wouldn't let them peek until they were in front of their very own home.

For the first time in years, Angel and Lester would have a place they could call their own. While Angel budgeted every cent and worked overtime, she fantasized about this day. Moving into a new home was all Angel imagined, though it was also sad to part from Gran. When Angel told Gran they were moving, Gran tried to smile, but cried instead. Gran told Angel she was happy for them. Gran loved having them around, but it was time for Angel to raise the children and repair her marriage without the comfort of knowing she could lean on Gran when things spun out of control.

Leaving the nest reminded Angel of how helpless she felt when she learned about Lester's affair with a woman whose name she tried to erase from her memory, but it popped in her thoughts often.

Seven months had passed since Pastor Davis paid them that unforgettable visit. Since that day, Angel decided to forgive Lester and forget what he'd done. She spent countless hours fasting and praying for strength to fall in love with Lester again. She desperately wanted her family to be happy and whole.

She studied the Bible and wrote down passages on forgiveness, so she could set those words before her when she wanted to walk away from the man who promised her the world in time. Angel and Lester never discussed Sheila or the baby after Pastor Davis paid them a visit. She never divulged the details to anyone but God. She didn't tell her sisters, friends, or even Gran what had happened. She swore to take the incident to her grave and prayed the children would never find out.

Angel threw herself into her career and was promoted to management. She started making substantially more money than Lester, who normally changed jobs every six months to a year. She became more active in church and tried to support Lester when he preached.

Whenever Angel was overwhelmed with the thought of Lester being unfaithful, she would remember how God forgave her when she was unfaithful to His commands and knew it was hypocritical to receive forgiveness and not be forgiving.

Angel was often invited to dinners with executives at her job, but she always declined with a flash of her wedding ring. She was making her marriage work and refused to be drawn into the cycle of do unto others as others have done to you. She desired more for her life and family than the consequences of being driven to please self. So she made the ultimate sacrifice and decided to always put her needs last. She held onto the familiar saying: Prayer changes things. And left everything in God's hands.

Moving from Gran's into their own home was a huge transition, but Angel thought it went well considering all the pieces that fit into the puzzle of becoming homeowners. Angel enrolled the children in public school and was pleased they adjusted to the new environment with ease and made friends in their new neighborhood in a matter of days. Angel stressed good behavior and excellent communication skills for Moses and Joy. She would correct them on everything from posture to placing commas properly in a sentence.

Since they no longer lived with Gran, the children were given the responsibility of walking from the elementary school to their house. The school was visible from their front porch. Joy was given a key and charged with calling Angel when she and Moses got home and making sure they completed their homework. They were home alone for two hours after school, since Angel didn't get off until after four and Lester went to church after he got off work most weeknights.

Normally, Moses and Joy got home and completed their homework without incident, but there were days when the two did not get along. As the older sister, Joy was left in charge and she always pulled rank on Moses. She shouted orders at him and when he did not comply, she would beat him up. Their arguments often ended with the two rolling around on the floor kicking, biting, and punching until they grew tired or they heard Angel at the front door.

When Angel got home she would start dinner and check homework. She was determined to be active in the children's education, even though she was extremely busy at work. For two years she ran the house smoothly without Gran's help, and thanked God for sustaining her. The time passed quickly and before she knew it, Joy was starting middle school and Moses was entering the fourth grade.

One Saturday afternoon Lester, Angel, and the kids were relaxing in the basement when the doorbell rang, followed by a hard pounding on the door.

"Kids, stay here while your father and I get the door."

"Yes, ma'am." Joy and Moses nudged each other as their parents went up the stairs. Once they reached the platform, the two stood at the bottom of the steps, trying to figure out who was at the front door.

As Lester opened the door, someone sped off in a car while honking repeatedly. Lester and Angel's attention was captured by the toddler sitting on their front porch with a note attached to his jacket.

I was surprised when I went to your church and discovered you were no longer there and had moved to the county. Pastor Davis let me know where I could find your happy family. This is your son, Jacob Noble. He deserves to live in a nice house like your other kids. It looks like our little secret is now your big problem.

Angel covered her mouth to muzzle the screams as her nightmare became intertwined with reality. "He looks just like Moses." Angel stood in shock as she stared at the crying boy, abandoned on their doorstep.

After what felt like an eternity, Angel snapped out of it and brought Jacob into the house, while Lester ranted about his mother being a maniac.

"Do you believe this nut?" Lester asked in disbelief as he massaged his forehead to prevent the pounding in his head.

"She isn't the only crazy person involved," Angel whispered.

"So you're taking the side of a woman who leaves her child on a front porch with a note?"

"I'm not taking anyone's side, but it appears this child is yours. I asked you if he could have been yours and you said no." Angel took off Jacob's coat and stared at his features.

"I thought we promised not to bring this up."

"Well, it's hard to ignore when I'm staring at the seed from the affair we're not supposed to say anything about." Angel sat down with Jacob on her lap, tapping her leg nervously. "It looks like we'll have to tell the family about Jacob."

"Tell them what? His mother will come back for him eventually. Until then, we're just babysitting."

"So you just act like you don't have another son? Is that what you're going to do?"

Before Lester could respond, Moses and Joy ran up the steps and into the living room.

"Mom, whose baby is that? He looks just like Moses." Joy laughed as she and Moses surrounded the baby to figure out what was going on.

"Joy, watch your mouth," Lester shouted.

"What did I say? He does. He has curly, light brown hair and his face is just like—"

"Don't say another word. Both of you go to your rooms for a little while. This baby was dropped off for us to babysit," Lester ordered.

Joy stomped to her room and closed the door, while Moses went to his room quietly.

"You know, Lester, when I took those wedding vows I meant every word."

"So did I," Lester interjected.

"Please don't interrupt. When I said for better or for worse, I meant that. This is for worse. I'm holding the child you made with another woman. I, your wife, have your child in my arms. I am willing to raise Jacob as our child because of my vow to God. It is nothing but God keeping me from throwing your things on the front lawn and changing the locks. I can run this house on my own, but I took a vow. I suggest you think about how you felt not having your father in your life before you think of not claiming Jacob."

"Angel, I know it may not feel like it now, but I love you. I love our family. I will step up to my responsibility, but I want us to keep this quiet for the next few days." Lester stood in front of Angel with his hand on her free shoulder.

"Here. Do you want to hold him?"

"No. I'm going out for some air. I will be back soon." Lester grabbed his jacket and keys, then shut the front door behind him.

For the next couple weeks Jacob was a part of the Noble household. Angel found a daycare provider for him while she went to work and picked him up when she got off. She was frustrated by Lester's hands-off approach with Jacob, and when she confronted him about his attitude, it always ended in an argument.

Lester and Angel told everyone the little boy was left on their doorstep. It was true, but not the whole truth. Most people didn't pay the explanation any attention, but drew their own conclusions based on Jacob and Moses's resemblance. Angel's family pressured her for more information, but she grudgingly stuck to Lester's story. She wouldn't ask for anyone's help with Jacob, because she was too embarrassed. There were times Angel wanted to cry on Gran's shoulder, but refrained because she didn't want her to worry.

To Angel's surprise, she was comforted by watching Joy and Moses play with Jacob.

"Mom, you can call us the three amigos," Moses joked as he held Jacob by the hand.

Since Joy and Moses often harassed Angel and Lester about having another baby, they told Angel Jacob was a blessing. Angel felt sorry for Jacob because Moses and Joy were obsessed with him. They tried to help feed and change him, but most of the time they just entertained him. He was a captive audience for the performances they put on in the basement, which Angel found amusing. Moses had a guitar he tinkered around with and Joy had a microphone. The scenarios were endless. Some afternoons, Joy was a singer and Moses a back-up musician, and there were times when Joy was a preacher and Moses was playing his guitar for the church choir. No matter what they decided to do, they would make their parents and now Jacob their audience.

Jacob's likeness to Moses was amazing. The two looked so much alike, strangers assumed they were brothers. Jacob's curly brown hair framed his chubby face like Moses's when he was two. Jacob was happy in the Noble home. He occasionally cried for his mother, but once Angel comforted him, he would stop.

Angel felt the strain of caring for Jacob more than anyone else. She tried to be everything to everyone, but was being stretched beyond her limits. When the phone rang on weeknights while Angel was in the middle of cooking dinner and reviewing homework, she cringed because she often felt like a suspect in an investigation.

"Hello." Angel balanced the phone between her ear and shoulder.

"Hi, darling," Gran said.

"Hi, Mom. What's up?"

"Just checking on you. You all right?"

"I'm fine."

"Who do you think you are fooling? You may be fooling everyone else, but you can't fool your mama."

"I'm not trying to fool anyone, Mom. What are you talking about?" Angel braced herself for the lecture coming.

"How long are you going to do this?"

"Do what, Mom?"

"Pretend like you aren't overwhelmed. Act like you aren't hurting every time you pick up that child and care for him. Pretend like Lester is not the devil himself, that sorry excuse..."

"Mom, please stop. I'm maintaining. Everything will be fine."

"How can you care for this boy and act like it's not tearing you apart? This is too much for you to handle. I'm sure Joy and Moses are confused about all this, not to mention feel neglected by all the attention you give to this mystery child."

"Hold on, Mom, someone is at the door." Angel placed the phone on the table while she walked into the living room.

Angel didn't like opening the door when Lester wasn't home, but since it was still daylight outside she looked through the peephole to see who was at the door.

"Is anybody home?" the woman on the front porch yelled.

While the lady rang the doorbell and pounded on the front door, Lester pulled up and parked, and Angel opened the door.

"Can I help you?" Angel asked.

"Yes, you can. You can give me my son." The woman stomped her foot and raised her voice to declare she wasn't moving until she got what she came for.

"Excuse me. What are you talking about?"

"Jacob is my son. I left him on your porch a few weeks ago with a note. I was angry at Lester and I wanted to get back at him, but now I want my son back. I came to take him home," she demanded as she moved closer to the front door, which was blocked by Angel.

Lester walked up the steps and stood behind the woman.

"What do you want, Sheila?"

The woman slowly turned around and locked eyes with Lester. "Not you!" She rolled her eyes and put her finger in Lester's face.

"Get your finger out of my face and get off my property before I call the police."

"Oh, you're going to call the police now? I will call the police and tell them you kidnapped my child. How about that? Give me my son."

"You can have your son." Lester brushed past the woman and stood next to Angel.

"What?" Angel whispered.

"Angel, please get Jacob and his things. This sorry excuse for a mother has returned, so he is no longer our responsibility."

Angel went in the basement where Jacob was laughing at Moses and Joy's rendition of Michael Jackson's "Beat It." As Angel scooped up Jacob she was relieved and sad at the same time.

"Where are you taking Jacob?" Moses asked.

"Just stay in the basement. I'll explain later."

When Angel returned, Lester and Sheila were still arguing on the porch.

"I'm a sorry excuse for a mother? You got some nerve, you deadbeat. You hadn't seen your son in two years. Trying to act like you are the perfect father and minister and you going to talk about me? That's how church folk do, always judging somebody else, when you should be looking at yourself."

"Here he is." Angel handed Jacob over to Sheila.

Jacob started crying as he left Angel's bosom and returned to the arms of Sheila. Jacob lifted his arms to return to Angel and started kicking and screaming. Angel ran into the house and locked herself in the bathroom to catch her breath for the wind that was knocked out of her the past few weeks and to cry for the little boy she nurtured and loved like he was born from her womb. She heard Jacob screaming outside and instinctively opened the door to grab him, but paused when she turned the corner and listened.

"Don't even start that noise, boy. It's your mama, Jacob. I came back for you," Sheila said.

"You take a nice long look at your son, because this is the last time you will see him. I'm getting married and my man and I are going to raise Jacob, so stay out of our lives."

"With pleasure." Lester slammed the door.

When Lester turned from slamming the door he almost walked into Angel, who was like a statue blocking his way from walking any farther.

"Are you happy now? Your son is no longer a constant reminder of your failure as a husband and father," Angel said as she lifted Lester's chin to make him look at her.

"None of this makes me happy. Especially you calling me a failure. Is that what I am to you?"

"Don't play the victim after all you've put me and this family through."

"I don't know how many times you want me to apologize, Angel. Yes, I messed up, but I want us to move on. She won't be back, so this won't be a problem anymore. That is, if you stop talking about it, we won't have a problem," Lester said as he fumbled for Angel's lifeless hand.

"I don't know if I can continue to do this with you." Angel pulled her hand out of Lester's sweaty fingers and ran to their bedroom for solace.

It wasn't until Angel heard the annoying dial tone that she remembered she left Gran on hold. Quickly dialing Gran's number, Angel told her Jacob's mother picked him up so she could stop worrying.

With Jacob gone, the house was back to normal. Angel missed bouncing Jacob on her knee and rocking him to sleep, but she welcomed the additional rest. She noticed Moses took Jacob's absence the hardest. He loved being the older brother for once and he instantly connected with Jacob. Joy missed Jacob, but she recovered quickly when Angel and Lester promised to take them to Disney World for summer vacation.

Angel was annoyed that Lester seemed unaffected by everything. He never emotionally attached himself to Jacob. He rarely held him and did his best to avoid looking into those eyes that were so familiar. Angel prayed Lester would do the right thing and fight for visitation of Jacob, but instead he tried to forget about him. He never mentioned him, though Angel knew his conscience would always remind him of what he was stealing from his son every moment he was absent from his life.

Three years after Jacob was wrenched from Angel's arms, she'd often spread the cream vertical blinds that covered the large bay window in the living room and stare like she was expecting him to appear on the porch. She thought about Jacob's well-being and wondered if he was happy. She wanted Lester to be in his life but wouldn't dare bring up the subject, since Lester was unapproachable when it came to discussing Jacob. Angel even considered tracking down Sheila and Jacob to see if he was okay, but knew it wasn't her place and feared the confrontation would do more harm than help.

Angel threw herself back into work and continued to climb the corporate ladder. She worked long hours and was exhausted as she was rewarded for her strong work ethic with more work. When she wasn't working she was running the household. She cooked balanced meals and cleaned when her strength permitted. She didn't have to keep as close an eye on the children, since they were getting older. Moses was in the seventh grade, and Joy was a freshman in high school.

Angel was relieved the turmoil with Lester seemed unnoticed by Joy and Moses. Angel wanted them to always love and respect Lester as their father; therefore, she tried to approach Lester about his behavior late at night or early in the morning when the children were asleep. He was employed on and off and it seemed more off than on. Angel thought he was disconnected from the family and tried to get to the root of the issue, but Lester never opened up. He responded with vague answers that never helped Angel get into his thoughts. She asked him if they could go to marital counseling, and Lester replied with an emphatic no. He wasn't hanging out at night, but since he worked sporadically Angel wondered where he spent most of his time. He didn't spend it cleaning, because the house was never clean when Angel got home from work.

Angel found it difficult to repair their marriage without demanding Lester check in emotionally. She didn't hound him when he was unemployed, as she thought that wasn't supportive. So she stayed in this place of observing her marriage instead of making it better because she felt her hands were tied. She searched scripture, prayed, and fasted to understand what her next move should be.

CHAPTER NINE

Joy began to blossom in her freshman year and was thrilled when the cumbersome braces that covered her teeth throughout middle school were gone and the pimples that plastered her face cleared up. She even convinced Angel to let her get a cute bob haircut for the first day of high school. Her transformation didn't go unnoticed as she got a lot of attention from guys, which was new to her. She welcomed the stares and smiles while she effortlessly adjusted to her newfound popularity. The only obstacle standing in the way of her soaring social life was Lester.

Lester's rule was supreme in the Noble home, and his decrees, though sometimes unreasonable, were final. Joy could not talk to guys on the phone or date until she reached sweet sixteen. For Joy that was the end of the world, because in ninth grade she was fourteen and she didn't understand why she couldn't chat with her male friends on the phone. Joy pleaded with Lester to change his mind and be reasonable. She even tried to get Angel involved in a tag-team effort, but he would not budge.

"This is not fair. Can we vote on it? Can everyone in the family vote? Raise your hand if you think I should be allowed to talk to boys on the phone and date now?" Joy raised her hand as a last effort to sway Lester.

"Listen, Joy, I don't know or care what other families do in their homes, but in this house we don't have a democracy, we have a dadocracy. The difference is, whatever I say is what goes."

Lester stood over Joy and leaned in so she heard him loud and clear. "There is not going to be a vote. This conversation is over."

That edict didn't sit well with Joy. As a result, the demise of Joy's desire to be daddy's little girl deconstructed while her desire for male attention grew. Since Joy wanted to date and talk to guys on the phone more than anything, she did what any average American teenager would do: she did it anyway.

Joy waited until late at night when the entire house was dark and quiet before she slipped out of bed and tiptoed downstairs to the basement. She knew what parts of the steps to place her small, pedicured feet on gently, so they wouldn't squeak. When she got downstairs, she flicked on the lights and called one of her male friends and chatted the night away.

Joy's plan worked for a while, until she made the mistake of giving the house number to her phone pals. Even though she gave her suitors specific instructions to never call her because she was so busy, they would still call. At random times a young man would call the Noble house asking for Joy and Lester would tell him she couldn't talk to boys on the phone. Joy wanted to curl up in a ball and hide in embarrassment when Lester said that to her friend.

The next day in school the guy would always approach Joy. "Why can't you talk to guys on the phone?" The grin on his face would be enough to make Joy want to crawl into the closest locker until she graduated.

Joy would shrug her shoulders in shame. "My father is strict, I guess."

Eventually, the guys got the hint because they stopped calling and Joy thought she had control of the situation again. Now all she had to do was stick to sneaking on the phone late at night and her social life would still have a chance.

She continued to wait until the house was completely quiet, except for Moses's snoring across the hall. Then she would quietly fold the covers back, slowly open her door, slink through the kitchen, and tiptoe down the steps.

Usually, the phone conversations consisted of general questions about school and what she was doing at the moment. The dialogue was never about anything deep. Typically, the conversations were filled with "he said/she said" comments and plans to meet at the movies or the mall. This went on for several nights before Joy noticed that when she was sneaking to the basement, Lester wasn't home.

For a while she thought it was great that Lester was out late. It meant she could talk on the phone and not worry about him catching her, but the fun faded when Joy overheard Lester and Angel arguing about the late hours he was keeping.

She overheard them bickering about why he was hanging out late and that Angel didn't know any of his new friends who seemed like trouble in her opinion. Angel told Lester he needed to be at home with his family. Lester's response was that his late nights with some fellas were harmless and he needed a life outside of the family. Joy didn't want her parents to argue and she wished Lester would stay at home like he used to, even if it meant she couldn't talk on the phone to guys at night.

Since Lester was never really home at night, Joy became relaxed with sneaking on the phone. One night she was sitting in the basement with her legs propped up on Lester's desk, talking to one of her guy friends around midnight. They were talking about the usual—nothing.

"What are you doing on the phone this late?" Lester demanded after he ran down the basement stairs like a herd of cattle was behind him.

Joy heard him before she saw him at the bottom of the basement steps.

"I got to go, talk to you later." Joy frantically hung up the phone and jumped up.

"Who were you talking to?"

"Just a friend."

"Go to bed."

She walked toward Lester with her hands on her hips, rolling her eyes in disgust. As she headed for the steps a stench odor burned her nostrils.

Joy paused and sniffed Lester's jacket with a nauseated look. "You smell like smoke."

Lester folded his arms as he did when he lectured her and shook his head like Joy had said something terrible.

"What the hell do you mean I smell like smoke? Don't you ever say that again," Lester yelled.

"Why are you yelling at me? You do smell like smoke," Joy cried out.

"Joy, you are really testing my patience. If you were in bed, you wouldn't be smelling anything. I am a grown man and that means you don't question me. Now, you should be glad I am not going to punish you because I know you were talking to some knucklehead on the phone when I told you not to. Now go to bed and cut all that crying out."

Joy ran up the stairs.

"Wonder what set him off. All I did was ask a question. He always gets upset over nothing," Joy mumbled as she stomped to her room and closed the door. She feared if she slammed it, Lester might go over the edge.

The next morning at school, Joy was distracted in social studies as she stared at the chalkboard while sitting across from her best friend, Tisha. Normally, the two would dish the latest gossip because it made class go faster.

"What's wrong with you?" Tisha asked.

Joy shrugged and took a deep breath.

"I think my father is having an affair," she whispered.

"What would make you say that?" Tisha asked.

"Well, he's staying out late. Last night he smelled like smoke and when I mentioned it, he got really upset. If he didn't have anything to hide, why would he yell at me? I don't think he's hanging out late with guys all the time." Joy's pupils were getting wet and she could feel tears welling up and slowly pushing their way to the front of her eyes. It was difficult, but she held them back because she didn't want an emotional breakdown in class.

"I know you aren't going to cry," Tisha said with a perplexed look on her face.

Joy sat slumped down in a chair, looking at her feet for an answer.

"I apologize for not being more sensitive to what you're going through. My mom and dad separated when I was young. I don't remember what it feels like to live in a home with both parents."

"I don't know if I still want to get married or not. It would probably just end anyway." Joy shuffled her assignment so their teacher would think they were discussing schoolwork.

"You can't live that way. You should live for the moment. Don't worry about what might happen. You can't control what is going to happen in the future. One thing I know is your dad loves you. I can't tell you when I saw my father last. At least yours is in your life. You really don't have any proof that he's having an affair. He could be hanging out with some friends and it's harmless."

"But he's a minister. He shouldn't be hanging out at all." Joy closed her textbook and whispered so the guy sitting next to her wouldn't hear her conversation.

"I guess. I don't know too much about ministers. The bottom line is you don't know if he's having an affair, so why worry about it? Now, if a woman calls your house and hangs up, then that's a different story," Tisha said, crossing her arms like she had made a closing argument for a major case.

Tisha's advice made Joy feel a little better. There was no reason to worry about things she could not control.

That afternoon Tisha and Joy caught the bus from school to Divas Beauty Salon in the city. When their stylist, Sherron, finished their hair, Joy called Lester to pick them up. After Lester picked them up they all got something to eat at a nearby mall.

They were cruising along Liberty Heights when someone started beeping a car horn. A black Mercedes Benz pulled up next to them and the driver motioned to roll the window down.

"Hey, Les, where were you the other night?" the guy said. "Mae had a slammin' party."

"I couldn't make it, man," Lester answered.

"Oh, well, I'm having a party at The Den on Saturday. There's going to be free food, Moet, all you can drink. Stop through."

"Thanks, man." Lester looked like a deer caught in headlights and shrugged.

The guy sped off while Joy was left in another uncomfortable position.

They dropped Tisha off and headed home in silence, while Joy played back the words spoken by the guy in the Mercedes. As Joy thought more about what had just happened, she realized Lester was doing things that weren't right. The mystery man in the Mercedes mentioned names of other people, a party Lester missed, and alcohol. It became obvious that Lester was living a lifestyle counter to that of a minister and faithful husband. Joy knew Angel should be made aware of what happened, but she didn't want to upset her.

Joy didn't think the events from the afternoon warranted getting Angel involved, but she thought it would help if she confronted Lester. When they arrived at home, Joy jumped out of the car, rushed into the house, and headed for her bedroom. She plopped on her bed and thought about what to say to Lester. A few minutes later she approached Lester in the kitchen.

"Who was Mr. Smooth in the Mercedes?"

"This guy I see out sometimes," Lester said as he finished a sip of Pepsi he'd just poured.

"Is he your friend?" Joy asked softly.

"No, he's just a guy I bump into on occasion." Lester put his glass on the counter and folded his arms as he faced Joy, anticipating her next question.

"Why was he telling you about a party at a bar? Why was he telling you about drinks?" Joy asked quickly in a slightly raised tone.

"Because he was. What difference does it make?" Lester snapped.

"It makes a huge difference because you are a minister and a married man. Why would you go to a bar? Is that what you learned in seminary? Did you learn how to smoke, drink, and run around on your wife?" Joy blurted before she could think about the consequences of her words.

Lester's eyes opened wide. He cocked his head and moved closer to Joy. He got in her face with his voice raised just below yelling.

"Who do you think you are talking to?"

"Who am I looking at?" she whispered after a long gulp.

Lester grabbed Joy by her shoulders, pushed her up against the wall, and looked straight into her eyes.

"You remember that I'm the father. I don't care what I do, you better respect me. Don't worry about what I do."

"How can I respect a man I can't stand to look at?" Joy cried.

She managed to get out of his grip and run to her room, frantically locking the door and turning on the radio. She knew Lester could have hit her and didn't want him to finish what he started. Angel was working late and Moses was hanging out with friends in the neighborhood, so Joy decided to stay in her room at least until someone else got home.

Lester left Joy alone in her room and never broke her door down to beat her senseless like Joy pictured when he pressed her against the dining-room wall. Joy knew her tone and what she said was accusatory and probably disrespectful. She didn't mean for the conversation to get out of hand, but she wanted to understand why Lester was going through so many changes.

Instead of confiding in someone, she passionately penned the details in her journal, the only thing that could hold all her secrets. After a few weeks passed, Joy tried to forget what had happened with Lester and not fret about what seemed to her like a mid-life crisis for her dad. But one afternoon in the school library, a classmate Joy grew up with since elementary school approached her about Lester.

"Hey, Joy, what's up?" Harold said as he walked toward the square wooden table where Joy was working on a social studies assignment with Tisha. Their table, filled with books, paper, and pens, looked like a tornado had crashed into it. "I'm glad I bumped into you. I've been meaning to ask you something."

"What's up?" Joy expected Harold to ask her out on a date or something.

"Are your parents divorced?"

"Why do you say that?" Joy said, her cheeks warm with embarrassment.

"Because your father doesn't act like he's married. I often see him around the neighborhood," Harold explained.

Joy was silent and didn't feel like discussing her parents with Harold. She sat for a moment and thought about a response that wouldn't cause her to cry in the library. As Joy prepared to tell Harold her parents were married, Tisha jumped in the conversation.

"Why would you ask her some stupid mess like that?" she said. "That is so inconsiderate; you don't know what she is going through. You need to mind your damn business." Tisha slammed her textbook down and stood up with her arms open, ready to fight, which caused everyone in the library to stop what they were doing and stare.

Their social studies teacher, Ms. Wallace, walked over and asked Tisha to come with her. Tisha hysterically explained the story to her in front of a captive audience.

Harold pulled Joy aside. "Oh, my goodness, I can't believe she is making such a big deal out of this. I didn't know; I'm sorry."

"That's okay," Joy said, wishing she could crawl under one of the tables and die from humiliation.

Even though Joy had told Harold it was okay, it really wasn't. It seemed no matter how hard Joy tried to focus on other things and not make Lester's lifestyle her problem, she was dragged into his mess. She didn't think it was fair that she had to respond to her classmates or anyone else about him not acting like a married man, not to mention a minister.

The last time Joy confronted Lester it didn't go well, and that was still fresh on her mind as she decided what to do about Harold's comments. She decided to be calm and respectful in her approach and was determined not to say anything sarcastic or sassy, no matter what Lester said.

When she arrived home that afternoon, Joy approached Lester about Harold's comments. Lester was on the phone whispering and laughing. Joy tried to eavesdrop before turning the corner of his make-shift office in the basement, but she couldn't make out his words.

"Hey, Dad, can I talk to you?"

Lester said goodbye to the person on the other end of the phone.

"Sure, what's up?"

"Today Harold asked me if you and Mom are divorced."

"Why would he ask that? You know we aren't divorced," Lester said calmly with a perplexed look.

"He said you act like you aren't married. I guess he's seen you out."

"Joy, what would some kid in your class know about me? People talk just to talk. I hope you aren't taking his comments seriously."

"Well, do you think you and Mom will get a divorce? Because you two don't seem happy and you do hang out."

"Joy, your Mom and I will be fine. I will try to stop hanging out as much, okay? I'll try to do better. Anything else you want to discuss?"

"No, that was it. Later."

Joy turned the corner and walked up the steps, not sure she accomplished anything by approaching Lester.

Joy didn't know what "I'll try to do better" meant, but at least Lester didn't scream at her like the last time she approached him about his behavior. Would Lester change? Joy prayed he would, because she desperately wanted her family to be happy.

CHAPTER TEN

There were days in high school when Joy would pull out notes she had jotted down during one of Lester's sermons titled "Don't Trust This." The sermon was taken from Psalm 146:3: "Do not put your trust in princes or other people, who cannot save you."

Joy thought it was ironic how the text applied to her relationship with Lester. As a little girl, Joy looked up to Lester and took everything he said as gospel. When he told her to do something, she believed it was because he knew best. But as she got older and learned the man she deemed a hero wasn't living the life he taught her to live, she stopped trusting him; she stopped putting her trust in people. She became guarded in her relationships and always questioned the motives of others.

Growing up, Joy thought preachers were above everyone else and could do no wrong. She even thought men of the cloth, who proclaimed to be called by God, had supernatural powers. When she thought of a preacher, the image of Superman came to mind. In the movies Superman was invincible, and used his power to help others. On the surface, Clark Kent appeared to be an average man, but when he stepped into a telephone booth and put on that red and blue spandex outfit with the big "S" on his shirt, and draped that cape around his shoulders, he became a superhero. Just like Superman, Joy understood ministers had regular jobs during the week and drove cars and had families like everyone else. However, when a preacher put on his preaching robe and stepped into the pulpit, he became Superman. Growing up, Joy thought Lester, as a preacher, had super powers that prevented him from sinning. But just like Superman with kryptonite, she realized preachers had weaknesses, too. She tried to stay as far away from ministers as possible, specifically Lester.

There were a few people she trusted and Angel was one of them, though Joy couldn't confide in her. Angel worked a lot and Joy admired her determination as a career woman, but she wished she was at home more. She wanted Angel to notice all of the things Lester was doing wrong and demand he change or put him out. Joy wanted Angel to stand up for herself, instead of finding solace in her career. Joy knew Angel could be strong, but she saw her tolerance of Lester as a weakness. She wanted to shake Angel, so she would wake up and realize she was supporting a man who did not respect her. She was supporting a man who didn't act like he was married. Joy knew the reason Angel didn't demand Lester change was because she thought that was not what a supportive, Christian wife would do. But Joy saw that as another way for Angel to hide from the truth. The truth was Lester was not supportive, loving, or a good example of a father, husband, or minister, and he needed to be forced to change. Joy thought the only person who could demand he change was Angel, but she wouldn't do it. Joy resented her mother a little for that because then Joy had to confront Lester, which not only made her feel uncomfortable, but put her in harm's way.

Since it didn't look like Lester was going to change, Joy decided to maneuver through life guarded. She thought that was the safest way to live. She placed a lock on her heart and threw the key into the sea of forever. She refused to fall in love. Though she had boyfriends and flirted with guys, Joy was determined to never share her heart.

She didn't know how to handle the destruction of her family, as it evolved from love to lies. Joy's family was her foundation. She wasn't sure how to move forward with it being cracked.

While Lester kept late nights, Joy was frustrated and pained that her father didn't care about her or their family anymore and that frustration created a void. It was like Joy had a black hole in her heart that she had to fill. She didn't know what it was, but it caused her to search for something. What she found was the need for more attention and decided to get it from someone other than her father—her boyfriend.

Joy liked star athletes, especially those who made her laugh. Consequently, she was instantly drawn to Marley, one of the star players on the basketball team. Marley was 6'9" with a medium build. His eyes were light brown, framed by thick, long eyelashes. He kept his hair cut close and always wore a gold cross around his neck. He always wore it when he played because he was convinced it was his good luck charm, though he insisted once he and Joy became a couple that she attend every home game because she was his true inspiration for playing his best. He was two years older than Joy, but since she was mature for her age that was never a problem. Marley was best friends with the school's star football player, Troy, a middle linebacker few messed with. Troy just happened to date one of Joy's close friends, Lalette, who everyone called "La" for short.

With Lester paying less attention to Joy's whereabouts, she was free to spend as much time with Marley as she wanted. Angel worked late, and was rarely home before six. Joy would tell her she was hanging out with friends at the library and that seemed to be all Angel needed to know. Since Joy started cooking, she would make dinner for the family a few nights out of the week to give Angel a break, while nobody noticed she was spending less time at home.

Joy managed to make the honor roll every semester. Excelling in her classes came easy, even though she rarely studied. Angel always held Joy to a higher standard academically than Moses, and when Joy confronted her about the double standard she said boys and girls are treated differently because it's harder in life for women.

Joy didn't understand why being a boy meant Moses was held less accountable for everything. He had fewer chores. He could date at a younger age. He could stay outside with his friends later.

He could bring home C's and not get in trouble. It seemed unfair that Moses got to do whatever he wanted while Joy had to fight for basic privileges like dating.

With Lester missing in action, his and Joy's confrontations about dating and curfew weren't as common. Angel always deferred the decision to Lester, and with his many disappearing acts Joy got her way by default.

It was bittersweet for Joy to see Lester's change in behavior. She missed the man who cared about what she was doing. She missed him asking what she was reading or writing. She missed the way he embarrassed her when he showed up at school and cracked jokes with her friends, but she loved her freedom. However, Joy was hurt more than she realized by Lester's absence. Joy was searching for something, yet she didn't understand why she had the desire to find comfort in someone else. She spent most of her time with Marley, since he made Joy a priority in his life and gave her his undivided attention.

"You know I love you." Marley smiled as he held Joy's hand while walking her to class.

"I know," Joy said.

"I'm for real. I know we've only been in a relationship for a few months, but I'm in love with you. You're different from all these other girls. You're smart and confident. I know you aren't with me because of what you can get, like all these chicks out here."

"I know, babe. I care about you, too." Joy kissed Marley on the cheek, hoping he wouldn't ask her if she loved him. In her opinion, he was moving too fast.

"You better get used to being called Mrs. Marley Harris, because you're going to be my wife one day."

"Can we graduate from high school before we start talking about marriage, Marley?" She wanted them to enjoy being in a relationship and not ruin it by talking about marriage.

"I'm sorry, sweetie, but I can't imagine us not being together." Marley hugged Joy, then left her at class and jetted to his session before the bell rang.

Marley always said just the right things to convince Joy he

would take care of her, although Joy tried not to believe in him because she thought it was safer that way.

Marley was used to women throwing themselves at him because he was a jock. It took him by surprise when Joy told him she wanted to wait until she was ready to have sex. A few months after making him wait, Joy decided to give in and replace her purity ring she had gotten from church with a promise ring from Marley. She did not have any expectations about what having sex with Marley would be like. After they slept together, Joy felt weird.

Joy tried to discuss sex with Angel on several occasions, but either she would cover her head with a blanket, act like she didn't hear Joy's questions, or give the same response: "Wait until you get married. I know you better not even think about getting pregnant!"

Joy knew premarital sex was wrong. She was practically raised in the church and remembered the sermons speaking against fornication. It was at church where Joy made a commitment to remain a virgin until her wedding night, but seeing her parents argue and Lester's lack of respect and love for Angel made her wonder why she should save herself for someone who would end up cheating on her. If it happened to her parents, she felt no couple was immune. Joy thought marriage was a joke.

Though Joy thought being with Marley sexually was a way to get back at Lester, it didn't make her feel any better. In fact, she felt worse. She thought she could handle being sexually active, but when she was alone, her thoughts were so loud she felt God was speaking directly to her and guilt overtook her. She recalled the words of the Approved Workman Are Not Ashamed (AWANA) counselor at church who drilled abstinence into her head at every meeting.

"A guy will not respect a woman who has premarital sex. He will never marry you. Instead, he will use you for as long as he can, get you pregnant, and discard you like yesterday's stinking trash. Trust me, ladies, I know what I'm talking about. Please wait for marriage," the instructor preached religiously to Joy and any other young lady within reach.

Even without the AWANA leader's voice blaring in her mind, Joy knew she was wrong. She couldn't even find rest when she laid her head down to sleep because it was then that her mind took a journey she could not control. All that she held in eventually seeped out in her subconscious. Joy's recurring nightmare involved her home and family being under attack by ninjas. The ninjas, dressed in all black, crawled onto the house, covering it from the roof to the ground. While they surrounded the entire house like ants consuming a dropped crumb, the Nobles were paralyzed with fear. They couldn't escape, so the family remained inside in the dark. Joy's body tensed as if she were living that moment of fear, and when it seemed as though the army of ninjas was going to attack, she'd spring up sweating with her chest heaving in and out, thanking God it was only a nightmare. Though she returned to reality with no physical scars, Joy was in spiritual warfare where the bruises weren't seen with the natural eye, but were far more damaging.

Joy felt her relationship with Marley was good because she cared for him, but thought they were moving way too fast. Joy didn't feel comfortable sharing the guilt she had about having sex with her friends because she knew they wouldn't understand. Joy wanted to confide in Angel about how her relationship with Marley had progressed, but wasn't sure she would be able to handle having the sex talk. All Joy could envision was Angel knocking her clear across the room when she mentioned the word sex.

Joy thought about it for several days and decided to tell Angel she was feeling down. Joy, not knowing exactly why she felt sad, found it hard to communicate that to Angel. Yet she wanted her mother's comfort. She wanted Angel to hug her and tell her what to do, and that although she'd messed up, she was still forgiven by God.

One afternoon, Angel arrived home a little earlier than normal. Joy thought it was the perfect time to share her feelings. Angel sat in the living room, reading her Bible, while dinner simmered on the stove.

"Mom, can I talk to you?" Joy sat in the chair next to Angel with only a small table and lamp separating them.

"Sure, what do you want to talk about?"

"Well, I'm kinda depressed."

"Don't ever say you are depressed. Christians are never depressed. There is nothing God can't handle. Don't ever say that again."

Joy took Angel's response as a sign she should keep her mouth shut and work her issues out on her own. She wanted to talk to God about how she was feeling, but felt guilty. Instead, she wrote her feelings on the pages of her journal and hoped the pages she confided in would give some perspective on her relationship.

I wonder where Mom and Moses put their pain. I wish things weren't so complicated.

Joy watched as Lester's late nights put greater distance between him and everyone else. Though Lester's behavior was not discussed, Joy felt the dysfunction in their home grow with every word that was never uttered. Joy tiptoed around the elephant in the room just like Angel and Moses. If nobody wanted to acknowledge the problem, Joy decided to keep her feelings to herself. Joy was consumed by the emptiness and pain Lester's being away from home caused, but figured nobody wanted to talk about it because that would open the wounds and everyone feared the exposure would do more harm than healing.

Joy worried about Angel and assumed the duty of watching over her. At night she snuck up the wooden stairs to her parents' room and peeked around the ledge to see what Angel was doing. Most times she would catch Angel kneeling by her bedside, praying, or laying on top of her comforter reading the Bible.

Even though she prayed about her problems, Joy knew Angel had another outlet. Though Angel rarely shed a tear in front of Joy and Moses, Joy suspected she let it out at some point. Sadness had to have entered her soul, but what she did with that grief was a mystery to Joy.

Joy also worried about Moses, who may have suffered worse

than anyone, because when Lester decided to cut out on Angel and the kids, Moses lost his father, his role model, and friend. At least Joy had Angel to look up to.

Joy didn't expect anything more from Lester because this was the man he was evolving into with every selfish act. He would often disappear for a couple days and return early on Sunday morning, just in time for church. Joy cringed at how they would all attend church like nothing was wrong and pretend to be happy and perfect. There were some Sundays Lester came in after staying out all night and preached the same morning. Joy sat next to her friends and listened to Lester, who she deemed as the phoniest preacher in the world. She'd get so upset she envisioned choking the life out of Lester, but Joy knew she would only get as far as lifting her hands to his throat before Lester would knock her out.

CHAPTER ELEVEN

As the family grew further apart and learned to live without Lester as an integral part of their lives, Lester fell deeper into the hole of misery he had created. His lifestyle did not bring him happiness; it only dulled the pain of his habits. He spent his time drinking the night away with *her* or other *hers*, as he was not committed to anyone or anything.

He tried to hide from God, but the spotlight of accountability would blind Lester when he ventured into nightclubs or hotels because someone always said, "I know you. Aren't you a minister?"

Lester would bolt out of sight and head for cover in the corner of a seedy nightclub or a cheap motel room, but he could not escape the presence of God. He thought if he drank more, got high, or filled his nights with meaningless sex, it would dull the deafening voice of conviction. As a man who studied the Bible inside and out, Lester sometimes laughed out loud at his attempts to hide from God. He knew God didn't just see his situation, but was also living inside him. Lester knew he grieved the Holy Spirit every time he defiled his body with drugs, drunkenness, and women other than Angel. When Lester awoke the mornings after his escapades, he would recall some of Psalm 139: "You have searched me, Lord, and you know me. You know when I sit and when I rise; you perceive my thoughts from afar. You discern my going out and my lying down; you are familiar with all my ways. Before a word is on my tongue, you, Lord, know it completely.

You hem me in behind and before, and you lay your hand upon me. Such knowledge is too wonderful for me, too lofty for me to attain. Where can I go from your Spirit? Where can I flee from your presence? If I go up to the heavens, you are there; if I make my bed in the depths, you are there."

Lester would then cry out in anguish to God in the wee hours of the morning. "Help me forgive myself and live according to the purpose you have for me."

Contrary to what Angel and the children thought and felt, Lester loved them, but the guilt he carried pushed him further away from the family man they once respected. While Lester's actions became less discreet, Angel and the kids were left to clean up the mess he had made of his life. They were left to answer the crank calls, deal with Lester not working or supporting them, and the rumors circulating around town about his late nights.

Lester was in an uncomfortable position in life. He knew his lifestyle was wrong, but the noise of living loose and hanging in dark places with people he didn't care about quieted some of the emotional turmoil he tried so desperately to escape. When he looked at his life, Lester saw the image of the man he swore he would never become, and this realization made him feel like he was buried alive.

It began with not being able to hold down a job. It was the subtle ways his family would respond to him when he was unemployed that made him feel like less of a man. He didn't feel like the provider or the leader; instead, he felt like he was leaching off Angel. That wasn't what he had intended, but something in him always snapped under pressure. His shoulders would always collapse under the weight of responsibility and he crumbled time and time again. He tried to fight the urges to quit jobs, but the urge always won with the desire to resign. He realized it was an unending cycle where he would have to explain to Angel he was no longer working and then look for a job again, when all he really wanted to do was be left alone to wander in his thoughts. As the resignations and layoffs became more common, he noticed Angel was progressing in her career and faith in God without him, and it hurt that she could do what he could not.

While Lester tried to find employment, he met women who told him everything he wanted to hear. How handsome and intelligent he was and how his wife was a lucky woman. While Angel's compliments of Lester were less frequent, he fell into the trap of other women. He knew it wasn't right to cheat on his wife, but it was what he needed at a time when he didn't feel worth much. Lester spent his time with women who stroked his ego; that's how he fathered Jacob. Lester was embarrassed by fathering a child outside of his marriage, but nauseated that he left Jacob to live life without a father. He couldn't forgive himself for that, and he felt like God was giving him an opportunity to turn everything around and do the right thing by taking care of Jacob and making amends with his Angel, Moses, and Joy, but he couldn't humble himself to admit he'd messed up. He also couldn't live with the decisions he'd made, and spent his time fighting the voices that told him he was worthless.

He watched the life he once loved and still desired as an outsider looking in while he stayed in the same spot and everyone else kept moving. He watched his family adjust to living without him. He watched as Joy ignored him and searched for attention from other guys. He watched Moses grow up and weave his way through the issues of manhood by himself. He watched as Angel's heart turned from him. He watched, but he never did anything to change what was happening to his family.

Lester came and went as he pleased. There were times when he didn't come home for days. This time the family hadn't seen or heard from him in a week.

"I'm going to call the local hospitals," Angel said.

After she called a few, Lester strolled in like nothing was wrong. Angel, Moses, and Joy were sitting on the bed when he walked into the room.

"Hey, guys, what's up?" he said. The grin was enough to make Joy scream.

"Where have you been?" Angel said.

"Out," he said without an explanation or an apology, and then shrugged his shoulders and went downstairs to the basement.

· · · · ·

Moses shook his head in disbelief at how Lester had changed. He couldn't believe his dad would stay away from home for days and not at least give them a call.

He reflected on their relationship growing up and how he longed to be like his father, but now he didn't want to be like him at all. He wished he could forget about him, but Moses couldn't go far without being reminded of him. In fact, all he had to do was look in the mirror to see he was a younger version of Lester. Moses was tall and slender like Lester as a teenager. He was fair with wavy hair he kept cut close. As he looked in the mirror it seemed like he was trying to see inside his soul, wondering if that was exactly like Lester's, too. He prayed it was not.

Moses was a young man of few words. He didn't say a lot, but when he spoke it was profound. Joy did enough talking for the both of them. Since he was a toddler, Angel was concerned about his quiet nature, but the pediatrician told Angel it was typical for the younger child to talk less if the older sibling was talkative. This proved true throughout Moses's life. Joy always did most of the talking while Moses did most of the listening. He was a great listener and observer, which was why he was very confused by Lester's behavior and the lack of accountability to Angel, his family, or the church.

Moses didn't understand how Lester could live like a single man and still reside in their home. He watched Angel suffer quietly and wanted to inflict pain on Lester, but was torn because he loved his dad.

Moses missed Lester playing basketball with him and taking him on the great adventures like he did years earlier, and he yearned to have those days back. It was Lester who taught him how to fix his tie, look someone in the eye, and protect himself if he ever got into an altercation. It was Lester who led him to

Christ when he was six years old. It was Lester who spoke life into his health scare when he was a boy and told him his faith in God was powerful enough to move mountains.

Now Moses was left to protect his family as Lester ran the streets of Baltimore. What made this responsibility worse was the only person they needed protection from was Lester. He didn't know what to do with Lester not being there; it was almost like his father had died. As he was coming to the end of his freshman year in high school, Moses had to figure a lot of things out on his own. He was dating different young ladies, as he did not want to commit to anyone. He knew that he never wanted to get married, and if he did decide to settle down with one woman, they would shack up, as he never wanted to be trapped in the hell called marriage. He'd seen enough failed marriages and he wasn't interested in making a life-long commitment that most people disregarded so carelessly.

Moses decided to stay away from home as much as possible. He spent most of his time riding his bike with the boys in the neighborhood. He barely passed his classes, but teachers never called with disciplinary issues, so Angel and Lester rarely pressed him about his less-than- mediocre grades. They never pushed Moses with regard to anything, whether it was academics, hobbies, or sports. It seemed that they had gotten lazy raising their second child. Where Joy had to fight for dating privileges and extending curfew, Moses never had any rules. This was often a sore spot between Moses and Joy. Moses wanted his parents to show more interest in his life, like they did for Joy.

With Lester's late nights, Moses started to wonder if his behavior was acceptable. He got up the nerve to talk to Angel about it one afternoon when they were alone at home.

"Hey, Mom, what's up?" Moses pulled out a chair in the dining room and turned it around, so he could face Angel in the kitchen.

"Not much, just making chicken stir-fry for dinner. What's on your mind?" Angel turned from the stove and smiled at Moses. He didn't normally start one-on-one conversations for no reason.

"Well, the other week when Dad was missing for days, I thought that was really messed up. I was wondering why you allow him to do whatever he wants. Is that how marriage works?" Moses asked, trying to get to the bottom of their issues without upsetting Angel.

"I didn't expect you to bring this up, but as a young man you deserve to know how a husband should behave. Your father is not acting like a husband and father should. We won't even get into him being a minister. Your father loves you and this family, but he's not reflecting that in his actions. His behavior is unacceptable, and as his wife I am praying for him. I can't force your father to do anything. I want you to look to God as the example, Moses, not your Dad."

"Why don't you divorce him?"

"Divorce is not the solution to a family's problems. What would that solve?"

"It would show that Dad's behavior isn't accepted."

"But how would that honor God? How would that repair our family? God is able to do anything but fail, Moses. I know you know that because God healed you when you were a boy. That same faith you had about being healed can apply to your father turning his life around and being here for us like he used to be. I know this is hard for you and Joy, but we'll get through this rough time. God can and will restore your father and this family. In the meantime, I want to make it clear that I don't condone his behavior."

Moses hugged Angel. "I'll pray with you, Mom."

CHAPTER TWELVE

Joy thought if she got proof of what Lester was doing late at night, that would provide some closure for her. She would use the proof to convince Angel to throw Lester out and get a divorce. Joy was tired of Lester slinking in during the early morning and still demanding she respect him. Joy had a plan to get the evidence she needed; all she had to do was execute it without getting caught.

She already tried to include Angel in getting proof by calling numbers back in Lester's pager, but Angel refused because she didn't want to know.

Angel responded to Joy's schemes the same every time: "It's in God's hands."

Since Joy knew Angel wouldn't approve of her plan to get proof, she decided not to let her in on the strategy. One night around eleven, Joy hid in the backseat of the family Lincoln Town Car while Lester went out for one of his evening escapades.

She crouched down on the floor of the backseat, curled up in a ball, and covered herself with a cream blanket that stayed in the car for when the kids took naps in the backset during their travels. It was a mild night in May, just a few weeks before summer break, so Joy thought hiding under the blanket was foolproof. She still prayed that Lester wouldn't catch her because Joy knew he would kill her if he did. She waited for what seemed like an eternity for him to leave the house.

"This will probably be the night he stays home. I should have brought something to read," Joy mumbled from under the blanket.

Joy was cramped and bored hiding in the backseat for over an hour. She was just about to give up on her plan when she heard the front door close.

Yep, it's happening.

Lester opened the car door and plopped down in the driver's seat.

Wonder where he's going tonight? Joy thought as she made sure not to make a sound even as she took short, quiet breaths buried underneath the blanket.

Lester drove about ten minutes before he put the car in park. He got out and Joy waited until the coast was clear before she lifted her head just enough so her eyes were level with the bottom of the window. It was hard to see, since it was dark. Joy had to squint to see her surroundings because of the glare coming from the lights on the parking lot.

After a few moments Joy realized she was in the back parking lot of the infamous Sinner's Den. Joy thought the name of the bar was ironically appropriate, and wondered if this was where Lester hung out on the nights he came home smelling like smoke. It was a low-rate spot not far from the Noble house. Angel would point out the establishment on their way home from church when they attended Bibleway, and warn them that only losers and trash went in there.

"Mom would die if she knew Dad was hanging out here."

Joy stretched out on the backseat for a few minutes to get some of the kinks out of her neck, back, and legs, then she crouched back into position. Forty-five minutes later, Joy's attention was drawn to the sounds of giggling and jingling of keys. Joy wanted to lift up to see who was giggling, but she wouldn't dare blow her cover, so she listened quietly to see if she recognized the voice.

"I thought you would never get here. I get tired of meeting you here all the time. I got to wait all night to get with my man."

"Yeah, I know you are craving for a brother. It took forever for my wife to fall asleep, but all I could think about was you."

I want to die. A sharp pain seared Joy's chest and she started crying silently.

At that moment, Joy wished she hadn't hidden in the car. She knew too much, and this was something she would not be able to erase from her memory. She also understood why Angel didn't follow Lester on his late-night trips or call the numbers in his pager. It was more painful knowing the details even if you already knew the deed.

Lester started the car and drove for what seemed to Joy like days. The initial disgust turned to rage and she wanted to blow her cover and scream, "You're busted," but she was too afraid of what would happen.

What am I going to do? Should I tell Mom?

The car stopped abruptly like Lester was about to pass his destination, and the half-drunk couple got out.

The thought of how Lester and *her* talked to each other made Joy so nauseated she cracked the rear car door and vomited on the street.

Joy woke up on the floor of the backseat, smothered by the blanket, to the glow of the rising sun. She looked at her watch to see how long she'd been asleep. To her surprise it was six o'clock Saturday morning. Joy felt just as bad when she dozed off, thinking of Lester's betrayal. Just the thought of Lester made Joy's skin crawl and her stomach turn in disgust. She opened the car door to vomit on the street, again.

Shortly after Joy closed the door she heard footsteps. Lester opened the car door and drove home. Joy finally had proof, although she never really needed it. After that night Joy stopped speaking to Lester and avoided him as much as possible. She couldn't stomach looking at him. The man who told her that lying to someone was the worst thing you could ever do made himself a liar to Joy, and she vowed never to forget the moment when her love for Lester melted into a memory.

Joy never mentioned her fact-finding mission or the evidence she gathered that night to Angel or anyone, but she intended to punish Lester by acting as if he did not exist. When Lester tried to talk to her she responded with shrugged shoulders. When he invited her to the movies or his trips to the library, she always declined. Lester even tried to bribe Joy with going to the mall, but to his surprise that didn't work.

A month after Joy's successful undercover operation, she and Lester had a run-in at home. She was passing through the kitchen to do laundry in the basement when she noticed Lester drinking a soda by the sink.

"What's your problem?" Lester asked Joy when she brushed past him in the kitchen. "Excuse me, Joy, I'm talking to you."

"Nothing," Joy mumbled and rolled her eyes.

"I don't know what this little attitude of yours is about, but you better get it together."

"What attitude are you referring to?" Joy put her laundry basket down, preparing for another confrontation.

"I'm talking about you ignoring me. I am your father and I'm tired of telling you to treat me as such."

"You don't act like my father," Joy said with her hand rested on her tiny hip.

"What do you mean I don't act like your father? I'm here, aren't I?"

"Barely."

"Joy, I'm not sure what you're trying to say, but the bottom line is whether you like it or not, I am your father. That means you will respect me. You will speak to me. You will stop rolling your eyes when you are in my presence or I'll knock those eyes to the back of your head permanently," Lester said sternly.

"One thing I can't change is you being my father, but I wish you weren't. I wish Mom would put you out." Joy braced herself, hoping Lester wouldn't knock her eyes into the back of her head like he threatened.

"That's not going to happen, so you better get your attitude straight. I'm warning you." Lester turned his back to Joy and finished his soda as he peered out the kitchen window.

Joy picked up her laundry basket because it was clear Lester was done with the conversation. She was fed up with Lester's late nights, his barked orders, and his laziness. Lester lounged around the house all day while Joy and Moses were at school and Angel worked. He wouldn't tell anyone he was laid off, but the family would discover it once they realized he'd been home all day for a week straight.

After praying about it and giving it much thought, Joy decided to confront the only person who could do something about Lester. For a few moments, Joy stood in the dining room and watched Angel prepare dinner and decided that was as good a moment as any to approach her. Joy had a way of cutting straight to the point. Most times she skipped pleasantries and started the conversation where most people would have eased the information in somewhere around the middle.

"Why don't you put him out? He doesn't work, he stays out all night, and he eats all the food."

"I'll let God deal with him," Angel responded calmly.

Guess there's no response to that approach. How can I refute God? Joy walked away from the conversation feeling like she would never wake from this nightmare.

CHAPTER THIRTEEN

With all of the problems in the Noble home, Joy was completely disinterested in her class work. It was easy to excel at Miller Academy because she didn't find the curriculum challenging. Joy spent class time socializing and daydreaming, but still made good grades. Joy found solace in hanging out with Marley or her girlfriends most of the time. If she wasn't hanging out with them, she was talking to them on the phone.

Although Joy never shared all of her family drama with anyone, she did confide in Marley and her friend La, who was a good listener and often shared her problems with Joy.

"Joy, I have to talk to you," Lalette bawled into the phone one evening.

"Why are you crying? What's up; what's wrong?"

"I'm pregnant. I don't know what I'm going to do. My mom is going to kill me."

Joy's mouth dropped as she looked at the phone like there was a bad connection. "Are you kidding?" Joy screamed in the telephone.

"I wish I was."

"Who is the father?"

"It's Troy's, of course. Who else would be the father?" she snapped after blowing her nose loudly.

Troy was La's best friend turned boyfriend. Joy thought they were a happy couple.

"What do you think I should do?"

"What do you mean?" Joy sat holding her head in disbelief.

"Do you think I should give this kid up for adoption?"

"Well, I've never been in a situation like this. It's hard to tell you what to do. I think if it were me I would keep the baby. I mean, that is a part of you, but it's your decision."

"Yeah, I understand. You're right. I can't give my baby away to some stranger. What if that family is crazy and takes it out on my child? Even though I don't have any money and my mother is going to kill me, I'm going to raise this baby."

"What did Troy say?"

"He wants us to get married after high school and raise the baby together."

"When are you going to tell your mom?"

"I'm going to try to tell her tonight. I might have to move in with you after I tell her."

"Funny."

"I'm not playing. She's really going to go berserk."

La wasn't kidding about moving in with Joy after she told her mom she was pregnant. Although La didn't actually move all of her things into the Noble home, she might as well have since she was at their house often. When La wasn't at Troy's house, she was at home with Joy. At first La thought Angel wouldn't let Joy spend time with her anymore because Angel was so religious, but she cared for La like she was family. Since he was never home, Lester barely noticed the new addition to the household.

One evening after school, La was hanging out with Joy at the Noble home. After eating the hearty meal Angel prepared, they sat in Joy's room on her bed as usual and talked about life. La reclined against several pillows propped up on Joy's headboard while Joy stretched out on the opposite end of the bed, flipping through a magazine. Though Joy and La had vastly different backgrounds, their friendship was solid. The two were always honest with each other. Joy didn't realize how much her friendship helped La through the rough times.

"Joy, you're a great friend."

"Where is this coming from? Are you about to ask me for some money?" Joy laughed at her own joke as she typically did.

"Girl, you are a mess. I'm serious. You've been with me through this pregnancy and you're always there for me when I need to vent."

"That's what friends are for. I know you would do the same for me."

"Joy, I love you and appreciate all you are doing for me. I'm terrified of being a mother, but I know God and I talk to Him about it. I know He will equip me with everything I need to take care of my baby. I pray every night that God will take care of us and have His way. I know I was wrong, but I have to take responsibility for my actions and turn my life around. This child will not be a teenage parent. I am going to break this cycle and be the best mother I can be." La reached for tissue as she mumbled into her cupped hands and leaned on Joy's shoulder.

Only time would reveal just how awesome God was in her life.

· · · · ·

The summer is the highlight of any teenager's life, and Joy was no exception. She, like any teenager, rejoiced when summer came because there was no school. Joy loved working during summer break, so she could save money for the things she wanted to buy. She never asked her parents for money because she had her own. On the weekends she went to the movies, shopping mall, downtown, to the park, and cookouts with her friends.

Joy tried to keep busy so she wouldn't focus on her family. She wanted a guy who would give her his undivided attention, and make her laugh at any moment. She found that in Marley. She spent most of her free time with him during the summer. His mother loved her and often called Joy her future daughter-in-law. That freaked Joy out because she didn't plan on marrying Marley. Though she cared for Marley, she didn't want to fall in love with him because she knew he would hurt her one day.

When Marley started talking about marriage and their future together, Joy stopped taking his calls and avoided him for days until she decided she'd punished him enough. Joy thought if they took a break from each other, Marley would stop talking about marriage all the time and just want to hang out. Marley didn't understand Joy's on-again, off-again attitude and chalked it up to hormones.

It seemed like the summer went extremely fast and before Joy knew it, she was going school shopping. Joy felt her senior year was going be her best year of high school, and couldn't believe she would be starting college in a year. She tried to block out how bad things were at home and focus on school, but it didn't always work. Joy and Lester continued to get in each other's way.

Joy had a private telephone line installed in her room when she got straight A's on her report card the semester before summer break. She asked Angel at the beginning of that semester if that could be her reward and Angel agreed. Lester didn't approve of Joy's private line because he couldn't monitor her phone calls. Though she was allowed to talk to boys and date, Lester still wanted to be able to eavesdrop on her conversations to see who Joy was talking to and what was being discussed. Since Lester couldn't pick up the phone and listen to Joy's conversations, he would periodically stand outside her bedroom door and listen as she conversed on the phone.

During the summer Joy talked all night to La or Marley on the phone. As the summer wound down, Joy got caught up with La on all the school gossip, so she would be ready for the social scene when they returned for senior year.

While they were chatting, Lester decided to put his ear against Joy's bedroom door. "Who are you talking to this late?" Lester asked as he cracked Joy's bedroom door open. "None of your business," Joy huffed. "Hold on, La."

"I'm still your father."

"Oh, you are? I can't tell. How are you going to come in at five a.m. some days and have the audacity to ask me who I'm talking to at midnight?"

Lester peered at her with an I-could-choke-you look, shook his head, and closed Joy's bedroom door.

Joy rolled her eyes then continued talking with La on the phone. "Girl, I don't know who he thinks he is. I am not going to put up with the 'Do as I say, not as I do' routine any longer. If he wants respect, he needs to respect us." Joy rolled her eyes and continued chatting until the early hours of the morning.

The week before school started, Joy had a lot of shopping to do. Moses didn't have a summer job, so he had to accept whatever amount Angel spent on his school gear. Joy, on the other hand, was a young woman with a wardrobe plan. She dragged Angel and Moses to every store imaginable until she found the perfect first-day outfit. Since it was her senior year, Angel and Moses grudgingly obliged and watched Joy model what seemed to be one hundred outfits.

"This is it! This screams, 'I'm a senior.' What do you think?" Joy asked, not needing their approval, but confirmation.

"Looks great," Angel and Moses chimed.

"Joy, I hope you put half as much effort into your schoolwork and selecting a college as you do shopping for clothes. Please get your priorities in order," Angel said with her hand on her hip, giving Joy that I'm-serious look.

"Of course, Mom. I've come this far, I'm not going to mess up now."

The first day of school went like all the previous years at Miller Academy, but Joy felt different because this was the last time she would have a first day in high school. She connected with her clique and they caught up on what they had missed since the last time they talked, which was just the night before on the telephone.

Even though Marley graduated and enrolled in a local college, he still managed to pick Joy up from school every day.

"Hey, babe. How was your first day?" Marley grinned as he opened the car door and gave Joy a hug and peck on the lips.

Joy returned the embrace with a limp hug. "It was good. Thanks."

"What's wrong with you?" Marley asked as he helped Joy into the passenger seat. Joy was familiar with the nauseated feeling she would get when Marley or any guy got too close. She loved him, but she didn't want to fall victim to being in love with him. She didn't want to ever be vulnerable to any man. It was time to give him the speech.

"I need to talk to you about something, but I want you to take me home first," Joy whispered.

"Here we go. Are you giving the speech again?" Marley pulled off and headed to Joy's house as she requested. They got there in record time.

"Alright, sweetie, I'm all ears." Marley put the gearshift in park and set his eyes on the girl he planned to marry.

"Well, you know I love you, but things are too serious for me. I feel suffocated and I don't want you to waste your time because I don't want to get married. It's not you, I just don't want to get married to anyone." Joy rushed her words and looked at Marley with the beautiful eyes he longed to see every day.

"Fine. I'm sick of this breaking up every couple of months because you have a fear of commitment. You need to grow up. I'm not going to keep breaking up and a few weeks later get back together. I want you to decide if this is what you want and stop sabotaging what we have. I love you. How many times do I have to say it? How many ways do I have to show you?" Marley leaned on the steering wheel, gripping it as if he were holding on for life.

"We can still be friends." Joy shrugged and opened the car door and hopped out, knowing that would set him off.

"No, Joy, not this time. I wish you the best. I'm a good man and I don't deserve being treated like this because you're afraid. We're not your parents."

"Why are you bringing my parents into this? I know we're not them!"

"Yeah? Well, you need to think about why you feel like this and get past it or you are going to be single for the rest of your life. Peace." Marley skidded off, leaving Joy in a cloud of smoke.

While Joy tried to clear her lungs, she thought about what

Marley had said. She wondered if she had a problem with commitment. Joy shrugged off his words and concluded that he was overreacting and she was too young to be in a serious relationship. Joy had more important things to contemplate, like her academic future.

In September, the Miller administrative staff encouraged all of the seniors to attend a college fair. It was held downtown in the Baltimore Convention Center. Hundreds of colleges and universities were expected to participate. The fair made Joy realize she didn't have much time to prepare for college.

Since Joy was in elementary school she thought Hillman, the college on her favorite television show, *A Different World*, was a real college. As a result, she planned to study at Hillman until someone told her the college didn't exist just a few weeks into her senior year of high school. Joy was heartbroken that she would never go to school with people like Dwayne Wayne, Whitley Gilbert, or Freddie Brooks. Unable to attend Hillman, Joy settled for the next best thing: a fun college with an inviting campus that was not too far from home.

Angel thought the college fair was a great opportunity for Joy to weigh her options and decided to tag along. Joy didn't mind Angel's company because she needed her advice and her approval on most of her major decisions.

At the college fair, the booths Angel and Joy saw first were for historically black colleges. Joy ran over to Gawson University and picked up a brochure. As Joy leaned in to ask the representative some questions, Angel frowned and grabbed Joy by the hand.

"That's enough of that. You shouldn't go to a black college, they party too much."

How in the world does she know that? Joy thought since Angel never went to college.

"Why don't you look at some universities out of state?"

They walked past a booth for a school neither one of them recognized, Hastings, and decided to double back. When they approached the booth, the admissions counselor was elated.

"Good morning, my name is Sarah Windley. I work in admissions at Hastings University. What is your name?" she asked while extending her hand to Joy.

"Joy Noble."

"What a beautiful name, Joy. Tell me about yourself. Are you an honor roll student? Do you play sports?"

"Yes, I'm an honor roll student, and if fashion is considered a sport then I should qualify for an athletic scholarship." Joy grinned and started laughing at her own joke.

"I see you aren't lacking a sense of humor. We would love to have you at Hastings. We're a small, private university, which enables us to provide our students with a quality education."

"Where are you located?" Joy asked.

"We're in Pennsylvania."

Pennsylvania didn't sound like an exciting state to Joy, but Angel thought it was great. The recruiter proceeded to tell them about tuition and housing. Then she said something that piqued their interest.

"We need more students of color. If you apply I know you will get a scholarship."

"That sounds easy enough," Joy said and nodded along with Angel.

"Here's the application, Joy. I'm going to waive the application fee. When you've completed it, mail it in the attached envelope." The admissions rep smiled.

"Thanks for the information. I'm going to apply."

"Great! I really think you'll like it at Hastings. It was a pleasure meeting both of you. Thanks for stopping by the table."

After the college fair, Angel treated Joy to lunch at The Cheesecake Factory. The hostess seated them next to a window with a view of the harbor.

"That Hastings sounds like a great school," Angel said.

"It sounded alright. I want to apply to some others including Ward University in D.C., since I'm the one who has to spend four years of my life at whatever college I choose."

"Of course you should weigh your options. Take your time, but not too much. Just make sure you don't apply to any universities in Maryland. Take my advice, I know what's best."

Joy let the college conversation end on the usual note—Angel's. There wasn't any need to argue since she hadn't taken the SAT yet.

In the beginning of November, Joy took the SAT with most of her classmates. She breezed through the language and writing portion, but struggled in the math section. The worst aspect of taking the SAT for Joy was waiting for her score. It seemed like months passed before she received the results, but in reality it was only four weeks. Joy was pleased with her results and so were Angel and Lester. Just as she expected, her math score was a little below average and her verbal score was above average.

"I'm going to college! This is the beginning of great things," Joy screamed and danced as she held the SAT letter in her hands.

CHAPTER FOURTEEN

La went into labor a week before Christmas. Angel drove Joy to Mountain Hospital where she was admitted. Joy was so excited La was delivering a new life into the world. It was an awesome responsibility and Joy wanted to be there as much as she could for La and the baby.

La gave birth to a beautiful, healthy girl. She named her Destiny, because La believed God created her to do great things. According to the doctor's diagnosis a few months earlier, Destiny would be mentally impaired and handicapped. Instead, she was born without any mental or physical problems.

Destiny looked like a tiny red doll with dark hair and dark eyes. She was beautiful, a perfect creation. Her mother, on the other hand, looked a mess. La's hair was all over her head and she looked like she had been beat up. She could barely talk because she was so tired. Troy was by her side, beaming from ear to ear. La's mother stood by her bed, smiling and staring at Destiny, while Troy's mother was in the waiting room with his friends and family.

La's mother apologized for mistreating her while she was pregnant. She was proud La faced her responsibility and brought her beautiful granddaughter into the world. Her mother was reminded that she had made her own missteps in life, too, and God granted her favor as a single mother. She believed if La trusted Him, He would do the same for her.

La was the wildest in their crew. She liked to party hard, but that all changed when she had Destiny. La and Joy often talked about God's purpose for their lives. La understood that Destiny came into her life at a time when she needed to slow down.

"I can't imagine my life without her. I would probably still be wild. Who knows what I would be doing if I didn't have Destiny to take care of. It's something how God works. Even when you don't know what to do, He speaks so clearly."

La loved being Destiny's mother. Other than her devotion to God, she was her priority. As a result, La was extremely protective of Destiny. She wouldn't let anyone babysit her. Eventually, La loosened up some and allowed Joy to look after Destiny occasionally.

A few months after Destiny was born, La and Troy broke up. Joy wondered if it was the pressure of being parents or if they just weren't meant to be together. Joy, being pessimistic about relationships, wasn't surprised it didn't work out. If adults couldn't make their relationships work, then La and Troy's relationship was doomed from the beginning.

CHAPTER FIFTEEN

As far as Joy could remember, Lester collected eagle statues. There were gold statues on his desk at home and artwork of eagles framed on every wall in the basement. Whenever he saw one in a store, he would buy it. As a little girl Joy never understood why he was obsessed with eagles. When she got older, Lester shared that he collected eagles because of his favorite scripture, Isaiah 40:31: "But those who hope in the Lord will renew their strength. They will soar on wings like eagles, they will run and not grow weary, they will walk and not be faint." He often shared with Joy at a young age the importance of not letting anyone prevent her from soaring. Even though Lester and Joy's relationship had dwindled to nothing, she kept the scripture close to her heart. She read it every night and it was a source of inspiration as she prepared to leave the nest to attend college in the fall.

The rest of Joy's senior year was pretty normal with planning her prom, graduation party, and college tours. She applied to five schools, two of them historically black colleges, and was accepted to all of them except one.

During springtime of Joy's senior year, she visited Hastings University in Pennsylvania and Mount College in Manhattan. Lester, Angel, Moses, and Joy piled into the family car for the road trip to Manhattan. At Mount College, Joy was ready for the school tour to conclude before it got started because the environment wasn't what she expected. She'd envisioned a college campus with green lawns, tall trees, and lots of large brick buildings.

In Manhattan the campus center was on one street and a few streets down was a building where classes were held. The dorms were scattered among different locations that were streets away from each other. Joy would have to maneuver through the city to find her way to class every day. She knew this was not the place for her and hoped the next college campus would be better.

The road trip to Hastings University in Pennsylvania offered more hope. The drive alongside mountains, trees, and rivers was serene, although Joy and her parents agreed something was missing from the scenery: black people. Then, just thirty miles away from the school, Joy saw a confederate flag flying proudly in the wind from a large house on the side of the road.

Where am I going? Joy wondered.

"Don't miss the exit, it's coming up. The sign read: Hastings University is the next exit." Joy tapped Lester on his shoulder to make sure he heard her.

"I see the humongous sign and I know where I'm going," Lester said and gave Joy the you-need-to-calm-down look in the rearview mirror.

Joy sat back in her seat, but watched to make sure Lester took the correct exit.

She felt compelled to highlight the obvious because Lester was always getting lost. On every trip he tried to find a shortcut and it would always take much longer to get to their destination. He never asked for directions, causing them to ride around until he finally found his way. Then Lester would pretend he took the longer route on purpose, so they could spend quality time together and enjoy the scenery.

Joy jumped out of the car. "This is beautiful. Just what I imagined a campus would look like. I'm excited!"

Inhaling the fresh air, Joy stood at the campus center and took in the tall, bountiful trees and beautiful green lawns that separated the residence halls and the academic buildings. During the campus tour Joy asked every question she could think of, except the one she was dying to ask: "Do any black students attend this school?"

At the library she saw a black girl working at the checkout counter, and smiled when they made eye contact. She had light brown skin, was about 5'4", and had short blond hair. Joy was relieved when she saw her, because it meant she wouldn't be the only black student on campus.

After the tour Joy took some placement tests and sat in on an informational session before the Nobles ventured back to Baltimore.

"I don't know if this college is for me."

"Why would you say that? It's a really nice school," Angel said.

"Well, I didn't see any black students in any of the meetings today."

"What about the black girl in the library?" Lester said.

"That's one black student out of one-thousand-plus students."

"If they give you a large scholarship, that's where you should go," Angel said.

"I guess." Joy slumped down in the backseat, hoping she would make the right decision.

Joy relaxed the rest of the ride home while Lester and Angel discussed her options. They even included Moses in the debate.

"It doesn't make a difference to me as long as I get her room when she leaves." Moses snickered and rubbed his hands together like he had a master plan. Since his plan was foolproof, he put on his headphones and listened to music for the rest of the ride home.

Joy weighed the pros and cons for all the schools and narrowed her choices to two colleges, Hastings and Ward. It was a daunting decision for an eighteen-year-old to make, but Angel and Lester let Joy decide, since she was going to spend the next four years on the chosen campus. Agonizing over what to do the entire week, Joy searched for a solution to her college dilemma. She had to make a decision, and she needed a sign to show her what school to select. Joy prayed for a sign, and at the end of that week she received one in the mail, in the form of a letter from Hastings University addressed to Miss Joy Noble.

"Hurry up and open it," Angel yelled as she peered over Joy's shoulder.

"Can you give me some breathing room, please? This is addressed to me."

"You better be glad I didn't open it. I have the right to open anything that comes to this house."

"Fine, fine, no need to get testy."

Joy opened the letter and read it to herself.

"What does it say?"

"Whoa, yeah, yes!" Joy screamed and jumped up and down.

"What? What does it say?"

"They awarded me a scholarship for fifty-thousand dollars."

"Thank you, Lord, thank you, Jesus," Angel yelled and jumped around the living room. "Well, you got the sign you've been praying for."

"Yes, I did get the sign I was looking for, Mom. Hastings University, here I come."

With all the excitement about college, Joy almost forgot about graduating from high school. It was impossible to focus with only a few weeks left in the school year. Joy's mind was already on her new campus.

Angel spent over a thousand dollars in preparation for Joy's graduation party, which bothered Lester because he thought the money could have been used to buy Joy a car. Joy became aware of the party details because she overheard Lester and Angel arguing over the expense like they did everything else.

The party was held in the Nobles' large backyard. Angel and her sister, Pam, went all out with the decorations. So much so, the entire neighborhood knew Joy graduated from the elaborate banners and beautiful balloons hung in the front and back yards. Angel prepared a feast and even bought bushels of steamed blue crabs for everyone to enjoy. Angel invited close to one hundred guests to celebrate Joy's big day.

The morning after graduation Joy expected to feel amazing, like when she walked across the stage and received her diploma. But instead she felt average. She was walking into another phase of life, but she didn't know what to expect. She was leaving her friends, family, and the only state she'd ever lived in behind. Some of her classmates decided to take a year off after high school, but that was never an option for Joy. Lester and Angel made it clear the next step after high school was college. Joy at no time felt like she had a choice to do anything else. Joy never lived on her own and she wondered if she would sink in the freedom or soar. The only way Joy would find out was to test her wings.

CHAPTER SIXTEEN

The night before Joy left for college, the living room was filled with suitcases, boxes, supplies, a television, a radio, and other miscellaneous items she managed to squeeze in as essentials. Angel invited her closest friends over for a small farewell dinner and they were amazed at the huge pile of things Joy was taking to college.

"Are you ever coming back home?" Wanda, Joy's friend from high school, shook her head at all the stuff Joy was taking to college.

While the girls ate and laughed, the phone kept ringing. When Joy would pick it up, the person on the other end would just breathe. It rang so much, Joy's friends asked who kept calling.

Holding the phone, Joy said loud enough for her friends and the caller to hear but low enough so Angel couldn't hear her upstairs, "Probably one of my father's hoes."

Joy laughed with her friends, but she really didn't think it was funny. When the phone rang again she played the "Bridal Chorus" aka "Here Comes the Bride" using the numbers on the phone.

"That's cute," a female voice said.

"What's your name, Miss That's Cute?" Joy asked.

She didn't respond, so Joy hung up and took the phone off the hook.

After Joy's friends left for the night, she and Angel spent the rest of the night packing.

"Joy, I'm sorry about the hang-up calls. I know it must make you feel uncomfortable with your friends around. I wish you could have had a normal night, laughing and enjoying your friends," Angel said as she wrapped her arm around Joy's shoulders and held her tightly for a few silent moments. "I'm going to miss you, but I'm so proud that you are going away to college."

"Thanks, Mom. Thanks for everything you do for me. I love you."

"I love you, too."

"You two still packing? Well, I'm going to bed since I'm driving tomorrow," Lester said when he came in at one in the morning.

Later that morning the Nobles and a few extended family members gathered to pack up Joy's belongings and move her to Hastings University. Before they pulled off, they gathered in the living room to pray for a safe journey. As they assembled in a circle, the phone rang. Angel's expression looked like that of a woman on edge.

Joy hurriedly picked up the phone and to her surprise it was La.

"I will truly miss you, girlie. I value our friendship and I know this is the beginning of great things for you. Don't forget about your B-more people. Destiny and I will be waiting for you to visit on breaks. We love you." La started crying.

"I love you, too. Talk to you soon." Joy hung up the phone and wiped her eyes, then joined the prayer circle.

"That was La wishing me a safe trip," Joy said as she grabbed hands and closed the circle.

While all heads were bowed and eyes closed, the family held hands as Lester started praying.

I wish someone else could pray because I don't think his prayer is going to get through to God, Joy thought as Lester prayed.

Joy wasn't the only one thinking that, because Gran squeezed her hand when Lester started praying and so did her Aunt Pam. When Joy looked up, almost everyone in the circle was rolling their eyes.

. . . . .

They arrived on campus at nine a.m. and drove up a steep hill to Joy's dormitory. The parking lot and residence hall were a zoo. There were family members fussing and ordering each other around. Little kids ran through the halls while the freshman students just went with the flow of all the excitement of arriving on campus and unpacking. Joy's residence hall wasn't air-conditioned; her family was dripping with sweat while unloading and unpacking boxes.

During the freshman convocation Joy took a long look at her surroundings, and felt like a foreigner in a strange land. She missed the comfort of seeing high school friends. She looked into the crowd for someone who would make her feel at home. With mostly white students in the auditorium, Joy felt alone. She'd graduated from a school that was predominantly black, and she took for granted the sense of belonging that environment provided.

I don't think I belong here.

Joy found her place and filed in line with her classmates. Lester, Angel, and the rest of the family were grinning so hard Joy thought their teeth were going to fall out of their mouths. Joy, on the other hand, was not thrilled.

"Pssst, pssst, hey girl, my name is Deon. I was so relieved when I saw you. I haven't seen any black people since I got here. Girl, I was scared this is KKK territory up here. We are in the middle of nowhere," Deon whispered after she tapped Joy on the shoulder ferociously. Deon wore her hair in box braids shaped in a bob style that framed her mocha face and highlighted her brown eyes.

"I'm Joy."

"Joy, I am not playing with you, girlfriend, we are in unfamiliar territory."

"I know, but we have to make the best of it. Where are you from, Deon?"

"I'm from Maryland."

"Me, too."

During convocation Deon tapped Joy every time she spotted a black person. That was the only reason Joy didn't fall asleep. The president of Hastings talked about diversity and how the school worked hard to create and nurture a diverse environment.

They need to fire whoever is in charge of diversity on campus, Joy thought from her seat.

Joy exchanged numbers with Deon and a few other students she met after the program concluded. She walked back to the residence hall with her family, feeling better since she'd met some people she could hang out with later at the ice-cream social.

The family voiced how nice the college seemed as they passed a fraternity on the way to Joy's dorm. Some of the frat guys were standing on the terrace of their building, holding up signs with numbers to rate the freshman females. They started whistling and waving when Joy walked by.

"I'm loving the freshman females," a guy said as he rubbed his hands through his blond hair.

Uncle Jefferson laughed and shook his head. "I can see they aren't worried about studying. Don't get caught up in the party life. Focus on your work, Joy."

When they got back to Joy's room it was empty. Joy was relieved that her roommate, Karen, wasn't around because she got a strange vibe from her. Karen was awkward and not friendly with Joy.

Joy, Angel, and Aunt Pam finished unpacking all of her things and fixed up the room, so everything was perfectly positioned. They did everything from hooking up Joy's brand-new computer to putting Yaffa blocks together.

"I guess we should go, so you can get adjusted," Angel said softly.

"Joy, I am going to miss you, take care," Aunt Pam whimpered.

Aunt Pam started bawling, which made Joy cry, while Angel had to console both of them. When they calmed down, everyone hugged and said goodbye.

"I am so proud of you and I love you very much. Call me tonight when you get back from the ice-cream social." Angel hugged Joy tightly.

"Okay. Love you." Joy sniffled as she waved goodbye until Angel and Aunt Pam were no longer in sight.

After a few weeks Joy adjusted to her academic environment and thought she could survive four years at Hastings, until she met the locals. When Joy shopped or dined in town, people stared at her like she had three heads. What was extremely insulting was when salespeople would follow Joy around in a store like she was going to steal something. Joy was convinced she couldn't endure four years trapped in a town where she didn't feel welcomed. Since she felt uncomfortable in the small town, Joy decided to return to Maryland and attend a university in state. The only thing she needed to enroll in another university was Angel's stamp of approval. Joy got up the courage to call Angel and tell her what she planned to do with her academic future.

"You want to do what?" Angel said. "I don't think so. You received that large scholarship. Things will get better. You know it's God's will for you to stay at Hastings."

Joy wanted to hang up the phone; she barely got two words in the conversation since Angel wouldn't take a breath. She tried to tell Angel she was unhappy because she was bored and didn't feel welcome in the town.

"Joy, life is not easy. When I started working for the government I didn't feel welcome to advance, but I did. Everyone is not going to like you. You have to find your own way on campus. You've only been there for a few weeks. You're not leaving and that's final," Angel decided.

So basically I should get over it. Thanks for the support, Mom, Joy thought and rolled her eyes and neck at the phone, like she was giving Angel a piece of her mind.

"Well, I guess I'm trapped here for the next four years. I should have never picked this school. Good night." Joy hung up the phone with an attitude as if that would make Angel change her mind.

Joy sulked after Angel shot down her plans to transfer and didn't call her for a week. Joy knew that wasn't going to change anything, so she decided to make the best of her college experience, especially since she didn't have a ride back home.

To make the best of the situation, Joy became consumed with schoolwork and extracurricular activities. There weren't any black sororities or fraternities on campus, so minority students created groups that they could call their own. One of the first groups she joined was The Sistaz—a group designed to give female students an opportunity to vent, bond, learn, and grow together. It was like a support meeting without the addiction component. The organization was open to all women, but was created by female students of color. In addition to joining The Sistaz, Joy also volunteered as a staff writer for the student newspaper, *The Hasty*. *The Hasty*'s advisor, Professor Chipper, took a personal interest in Joy's academic career, and became her unofficial academic advisor.

Joy's first-semester classes were brutal; she'd never worked so hard in her life. She was accustomed to breezing through assignments in high school, but quickly learned her old study habits wouldn't make the grade in college. Professor Washington was one of five African-American faculty members on campus. Joy thought he looked too young and cool to be a professor, but he made it clear by his tone and syllabus that he didn't play and this wouldn't be an easy course. The first day of class opened with a pop quiz. The first question asked was, "Is Egypt in Africa?"

This has to be a trick question, Joy thought as she marked no.

Needless to say, she failed the first pop quiz and learned that Egypt was in Africa. Professor Washington assigned work like his class was the only one anyone was taking. He assigned *Sundiata* by D.T. Niana and *Things Fall Apart* by Chinua Achebe as reading assignments on oral traditions in the African community, along with a fifteen-page paper the first month of class, and gave a massive exam the next month. Joy's friends couldn't believe her workload.

When Joy's first paper for African History class was returned, it had so much red ink on it she was surprised and relieved she got a C+. Professor Washington told Joy he saw enormous potential in her and offered advice on improving her writing and research skills. Joy took all of his advice and worked diligently on her assignments. She even delved into some grammar guidebooks for help.

In a short time Joy improved tremendously in all her classes, so much that she made the freshman honor roll her first semester. Lester and Angel were so proud of her grades they drove to Hastings for the ceremony, and took Joy to dinner afterward to celebrate. Joy studied Angel and Lester's interaction throughout dinner to gauge if their marriage had improved since she started school or continued its downward spiral to a pre-divorce state. They seemed the same, which meant they had problems, but they were putting on a united front for Joy. They weren't affectionate, but Joy was used to that, since she hadn't seen them kiss in years. She couldn't remember the last time she saw them hug or hold hands. Their relationship seemed like it was barely surviving out of convenience. Joy didn't understand why they were still together because she and Moses were old enough to handle a divorce. If Angel and Lester wanted to continue the charade, Joy was not going to get in their way.

During Joy's freshman year, Lester and Angel participated in all the family activities on campus, driving up for family weekend, homecoming, and any other events they read about in the school newspaper. Angel subscribed to the *Hasty* so she could read Joy's articles and share them with friends, family, and coworkers.

When Lester and Angel arrived for family weekend on the first Saturday in October, Joy greeted them with a big hug.

"Can you tell I gained weight?" Joy asked as she turned around and posed with her arms folded.

"You look the same," Angel said while Lester nodded in agreement.

"I gained fifteen pounds! I can't fit into my jeans anymore. We'll have to go shopping for some new pants, since I can't fit into my old ones."

"Wow, fifteen pounds in just a couple months. I can't tell; you look great! I missed you so much," Angel said and hugged Joy like she hadn't just seen her a couple weeks earlier.

After breakfast in the cafeteria they strolled through the town shopping mall and then attended the football game. Hastings was a NCAA Division III Mid-Atlantic Conference school. Typically, D3 schools are smaller than D1 and don't provide scholarships to athletes for playing a sport. As a result, the football games weren't that intense like the coveted events at D1 colleges. The best part of the game was when the Hastings Hawk would pump up the crowd. The Hastings Hawk always delivered an extraordinary performance. While the Hawk ran up and down the bleachers like he was on fire, the crowd jumped on its feet and roared with excitement.

In the evening the family enjoyed the school's fall musical production, *Little Shop of Horrors*, then concluded the night with dinner at a local restaurant. At the end of the meal Lester went to get the car; he always managed to exit when the bill came. While he was gone, Angel grabbed Joy's arm.

"Please stay in the hotel room with us," Angel begged.

"I don't want to impose on you guys."

"Please, I don't want any private time with him. I came up here to see you. We aren't getting close anymore and I want to keep it that way."

"Alright, I'll stay with you." Joy didn't mind staying with her parents, especially if it made Angel more comfortable.

The next morning the family went to church in the campus chapel. The service was a lot drier than they were accustomed to. The church didn't have a choir; instead, the audience sang from a hymn book while the organist played. The chaplain was good, but he didn't get emotional like the preachers from Baltimore. He delivered the sermon without hooping or hollering. Joy thought it was a different approach, one that often led to her daydreaming.

Before Angel and Lester returned home they dined in the campus cafeteria. Joy enjoyed their visit, but was ready for them to leave. She'd grown tired of the deafening silence among her parents and was drained from entertaining them all weekend. She even wished Moses would have tagged along for the trip, so she wouldn't be the only person running interference in her parents' weird relationship. Joy didn't blame Moses for declining the invitation to visit for family weekend because she knew he needed an escape from living with Lester and Angel. He said he had to work, but Joy knew he didn't want to come.

CHAPTER SEVENTEEN

Angel turned up the Christian radio broadcast while the speaker of the hour talked about broken marriages. Joy could tell Lester and Angel's relationship was getting worse when they picked her up for Thanksgiving break, because on the ride home they barely said two words to each other.

At the end of his radio segment, the preacher asked listeners to pray for their spouse who was living in sin. Angel grabbed Lester's right hand while he steered the wheel with his left. Lester appeared shocked by the gesture, but didn't say a word. They rode the rest of the way home in silence other than the music playing on the Christian radio station. When they arrived at home, Joy smiled at how everything looked the same. She hopped out of the car, unloaded her luggage, and ran inside to call her friends.

"What's up?" Moses managed to break away from his video games to speak and grab something from the refrigerator.

"Nothing much. Things are going well at school," Joy said, standing in the kitchen.

"That's cool. So you think you're going to stay there for four years?"

"Yeah, I really don't have a choice. I wanted to transfer to a school in Maryland in my first semester, but Mom wasn't hearing it, so I stayed. Now I like it and I'll finish there and see what's next. How is school for you? Are you thinking about what college you want to go to?"

"School is okay. I'm going to pass. As far as college, I want to go away, but we'll see where I get in; maybe a school in Virginia."

"Sounds good. So how are Mom and Dad?"

"They're the same. Dad comes and goes as he pleases and Mom doesn't say anything about it, at least that's what I've observed. You were always better at eavesdropping than me. I can't wait to move out. This can't be what life is supposed to be like when you become an adult. I never want to live like them. I'm never getting married."

"I understand what you mean. Well, the holiday should be interesting. I'll catch up with you later." *After growing up in this family, I can see why neither one of us would ever get married.* Joy went to her room and unpacked.

The first few days of her break, Joy was amazed that Lester stayed home, even if it was just for the holiday.

Thanksgiving was a big holiday for Joy's extended family. Most of Angel's siblings, their spouses, and children gathered to eat great food and enjoy fellowship with each other. The Nobles hosted this year's dinner. Angel started cooking the night before and finished the next afternoon. She decorated the house in autumn colors and Joy teased Angel, saying she was a down-to-earth version of Martha Stewart and called her Mama Stewart because she wouldn't rest until everything was perfect.

That evening Joy's friend Renee called and asked if she wanted to go to the mall with her the next day for Black Friday, since everything would be on sale. Joy loved to shop, so naturally she agreed to the retail therapy. When the phone rang early the next morning, Joy knew it was Renee.

"Yes, Renee, I'm up."

"Your father is a liar," *she* said.

Because *she* hung up quickly, Joy didn't get a chance to respond. Instead, she slammed the phone down and ran upstairs looking for Angel. When Joy realized Angel wasn't home, she decided to tell Lester what *she* said on the phone. After Joy told Lester what had happened, he dashed out the front door. When he came back about an hour later, Lester had a huge cut on his face. Joy didn't want to know what he'd done or what had happened, so she went in her room and got ready to go out with Renee.

Like most school breaks, Thanksgiving was too short for Joy. During the drive back to school, nobody spoke. The only person talking was the DJ on the Christian radio station Angel listened to faithfully. Joy hated listening to that station because they talked for most of the program. When they did play music it sounded like opera, which was not Joy's preference. She started to ask Angel to put in a gospel tape, but then decided to go to sleep instead and tune out the radio and the couple's awkward silence.

When they arrived at the dorm, Joy rushed out of the car like she was being released from captivity.

"No need to walk me to my room. I'm fine. Thanks for driving me." After hugging Angel and Lester goodbye, Joy grabbed her suitcase and darted to her dorm room.

Once again Joy was relieved to enter her dorm room. She would try to forget her family issues and get back to just being a student. She knew when Christmas break came around she'd miss her family again and be ready to go back home.

· · · · ·

As a little girl, Joy would watch Angel bake chocolate chip cookies for Santa Claus on Christmas Eve. It was Joy's job to put the cookies on a small white plate and set them on the table next to a tall glass of milk near the front door. Angel told Joy and Moses that would help them get the toys on their Christmas list. After placing the cookies on the table, Joy would run up the stairs to her room, jump in bed, and bury her head on a pillow before dark, hoping the next day would come fast. Moses wasn't far behind because he wanted Christmas to come fast, too. When Moses and Joy ran upstairs there were no presents under the tree, but when they woke up at dawn the next day the entire living room was filled with toys and clothes. One year Angel and Lester gave them matching Michael Jackson red pleather jackets, a white glove for each of them, and Michael Jackson record players. Moses and Joy danced on their toes and did the moonwalk while singing "heehee" and "chamon" for most of the morning.

Now the days of gathering around the Christmas tree as a family seemed far-reaching, since Lester rarely stayed at home, and though Christmas was one of Joy's favorite holidays she dreaded the day because it would not be the same as years past. She would exchange the presents for Lester's presence, not just physically but emotionally. She wanted him to check back in their lives. She wanted him to care.

During the first few days of Joy's winter break, Lester stayed at home, then one morning Joy overheard Angel pleading with Lester.

"Can you stay home at least for the holiday? If you can't respect and honor me, at least respect the children. It's Christmas," Angel whispered.

Angel's request didn't receive a response, at least not one Joy overheard as she eavesdropped from her bedroom. She only heard the door slam and Lester walking down the steps to the car and driving off.

On Christmas Eve, Angel, Moses, and Joy searched for a Christmas tree. It was a sad sight, because all of the good trees were gone and the pickings were slim. Most of the trees left looked worse than that pathetic tree Charlie Brown decorated every year on television. After two hours of searching in frigid weather, they finally found a decent tree. By this time their fingers were numb. Both Joy and Moses were so ready to go home, they didn't even argue. That was one of Angel's cues that the two were at their breaking point. Normally, they could argue about anything non-stop, so when they stopped speaking it was time to call it quits.

Angel held the tree in front, while Joy held the middle and Moses carried the weight at the end. The three of them carried the tree into the house and secured it in the base, relieved that they made it inside without incident. After hanging their coats and fixing hot chocolate, they put in Kirk Franklin and the Family's Christmas CD and started trimming the tree. As usual, Moses managed to disappear once they put the lights on. Angel and Joy finished decorating the tree around eleven that night and there was still no sign of Lester.

"I wonder where Dad is," Joy said.

Angel frowned and shrugged her shoulders. "I don't know."

"How could he be hanging out at Christmas?" Joy shook her head.

"We can't worry about what your father is doing. Let's make the best of the holiday. Finish wrapping your gifts and I'll see you early in the morning."

Joy went to her room and finished wrapping the presents she bought. Most of the gifts were for Angel because Joy thought if she showered her with nice things, it would make her feel better. On the other hand, Joy decided not to buy Lester anything. She was tired of pretending like she wasn't bothered by his behavior and tried to hurt him any way she could. Joy knew that wasn't right, and it didn't make her feel better, but she wanted to communicate with Lester what she couldn't put into words: she was tired of pretending.

Joy awoke the next morning to the aroma of lemon pound cake, sweet potatoes, and honey ham. With her eyes still closed, Joy smiled when she realized it was Christmas morning and there were gifts under the tree. Joy entered the living room, surveyed the boxes with her name on them, then peeked in the kitchen where Angel was cooking and singing along with Christmas songs on the radio.

Since Joy was in the holiday spirit, she decided to include Lester in the gift-opening production, so she ran upstairs to wake him. When she reached the top of the steps she slid over to their bed, as she loved sliding in her socks across the wood floor. When she plopped down on the bed Joy noticed Lester wasn't in it. She ran downstairs and looked in the basement—he wasn't there either.

I can't believe he abandoned us on Christmas.

She sulked on the sofa for about a half hour before Angel yelled down the steps.

"Joy, come up here and open your presents."

She stomped up the steps and heeded her mother's wishes.

"Do you know where Dad is?"

"No, I don't. Do I ever know where your father is?"

Angel ran into Moses's room and jumped on his bed. "Time to open gifts."

The three of them sat in the living room and opened gifts. Angel was kind enough to write *From Mom and Dad* on all the presents, even though Joy knew better. They tore the wrapping paper off the boxes like there was a million dollars tucked inside each one.

They got so caught up in opening gifts, before they knew it people were pounding on their front door and ringing the doorbell.

Aunt Pam, Gran, and Aunt Emma were the first guests to arrive. When Gran walked in she smiled and gave Moses and Joy a big hug.

"The house is beautiful, look at that tree. Who decorated the tree?" Gran asked.

"Mom and I did." Joy smiled. "Oh, and Moses helped a little."

"It looks like a professionally decorated tree. Well, enough about the tree. I'm ready to eat. Where is your father?" Gran said.

"I haven't seen him," Joy replied.

"What?" she said in a high-pitched tone. "Dirty dog; God is going to fix him."

Joy didn't know how God was going to fix Lester, but she prayed that He wouldn't let anyone else ask, "Where is your father?" She also prayed Angel wouldn't have a nervous break-down during dinner. It was their family tradition to gather in a circle, hold hands, and pray before holiday meals. Lester would always say the grace. In his absence, Angel asked Uncle Jefferson to bless the food.

With their heads bowed and eyes closed, Uncle Jefferson cleared his throat and parted his lips to pray. Before he could say "Let us pray," the front door screeched open and slammed shut.

"Merry Christmas, everybody! Y'all weren't going to eat without me, were you?" Lester said with a stupid grin on his face.

Angel looked like she was going to burst into tears.

Lester made a space for himself in the circle. "Let's say grace," he said.

Joy was standing between Gran and Aunt Pam. While Lester prayed, she could feel both of them squeezing her hands. Joy knew everyone was probably doing the same thing. When Lester finished praying, the macaroni and cheese could be heard bubbling in the next room. There was nothing left to say, but "Let's eat."

Everyone rushed to the back room where the food was set up. One of the cousins almost knocked Gran over, trying to get in the front of the line.

"Wait a minute, everybody freeze," Aunt Pam said. "Gran fixes her plate first, so everybody else back up." She held a paper plate up as a shield and a plastic knife as a sword to keep the hungry crowd at bay.

There was some mumbling and moaning, but not one person dared to complain out loud about Gran fixing her plate first.

Lester went into the other room to watch television. Joy noticed he was fidgeting like he had other plans.

Once everyone fixed their plates, sat down, and started eating, the only sounds heard were chomping, smacking lips, and gulping. After the first round, some people went back for seconds, while others leaned back in their chairs and unbuttoned their belts a notch.

"Make sure you leave room for dessert," Joy said.

Joy had spent a good portion of the previous day baking; she wanted to make sure everyone tasted at least one of the desserts she had prepared. She also wanted to speed up the dinner process, so they could exchange gifts.

Everyone rushed around, getting their presents in order for the grand gift exchange. Joy was pleased with the gifts she received, especially her favorite—money. In Joy's opinion, it was the best gift because she never had to return or exchange money.

It was always the right size, style, and color. When she finished opening her cards and gifts, she gathered everything together and stared at her bounty. It was a nice chunk of change for a college student. She looked around the room to make sure nobody was watching her treasures, then gathered her gifts and went to her room to hide her loot. Assuming she was alone, Joy didn't close her door.

Joy counted the cash again before she hid it under her mattress. As soon as she finished hiding it she saw someone walk past her room. When Joy peeked around the corner she noticed Lester walk away, which seemed strange, but she shrugged it off as nothing.

The party started to wind down around nine. Joy was exhausted and dreaded cleaning up the basement and kitchen. When she finished cleaning around midnight, all she wanted to do was fall into bed and sleep the night and next day away. The only thing that gave her a burst of energy was the four hundred dollars sandwiched between her mattress and box spring.

Joy reached underneath the mattress to count her money once more before she went to bed, but didn't feel it. She ran her hand along the entire side of the mattress to see if it had slipped down. When she still couldn't feel it she lifted up the entire mattress.

"Somebody ripped me off!"

Joy couldn't imagine any of their dinner guests stealing from her. The only culprit she could think of was Lester.

How could Dad steal my Christmas money?

The more Joy thought about Lester spending her money, the more enraged, hurt, and disgusted she became. All she could do was fall to the floor and sob. She wanted to cut him deep, so she grabbed the only weapon she owned, her Bible, and searched for something to pierce him like he'd crushed her.

She sat on the floor and thumbed through the books of the Bible like her fingers were on fire. She wrote the scriptures she found on a sheet of white paper in red permanent marker. Below the verses she wrote three sentences in bold letters.

Four hundred dollars stolen. Would a father steal from his child? Yes!

She posted the note on one of his favorite things, the refrigerator.

Joy crawled underneath the covers, closed her eyes, and cried herself to sleep. Several hours later Lester knocked on her door.

"Come in." Joy rolled her eyes, wondering what Lester would say.

Lester flicked on the bedroom light and rushed toward her. Tears fell down his face as he gripped the note in his left hand.

"Joy, what is this about?" Lester asked.

"Someone stole my Christmas money. Four hundred dollars!" Joy snapped.

"You think I stole it? I would never steal from you. It was probably one of your cousins, or maybe Moses stole the money."

Lester's speech was convincing, and made Joy second-guess her conclusion about the missing money. Later that morning she told Angel what had happened. Angel told Joy she was convinced Lester stole the money. She replaced the four hundred dollars and insisted Joy put the money in her bank account as soon as possible.

The days after Christmas were uncomfortable. What made it worse for Joy was how Lester acted as if everything was great. He pretended Joy never accused him of stealing. Meanwhile, he continued preaching.

On New Year's Eve, Joy prepared to return to campus. She pulled out her hamper filled with dirty clothes and started washing.

Joy was in the laundry room taking clothes from the washing machine and dumping them in the dryer when she noticed a clear small bag in the dryer. It looked like a tiny Ziploc bag, but it was too small to store food. Lester's clothes were in the dryer last, so she figured the bag fell out of one of his pockets. Joy took the bag upstairs and showed Angel what she'd found. When she gave the bag to her, Angel turned at least five different colors. Joy wasn't sure of the contents since the bag was empty, but the look on Angel's face meant things were worse than she thought.

"What do you think was in here?" Joy asked.

"I don't know, Joy. Honestly, I don't want to know, but I'll deal with your father. Don't say anything to him about what you found," Angel said.

"Okay." Joy rolled her eyes, wondering how much more Angel was going to take from Lester.

When winter break ended Joy was more than ready to return to school. She actually looked forward to her classes. Once again she was looking forward to anything that distanced her from Lester. Though she was excited about going back to school, her heart ached for Angel. Joy felt like she needed to protect Angel from Lester. She needed to protect her from his late nights, the crank calls, and the secrets that plagued their home, but she felt helpless. The only thing Joy could do was pray, and that she did.

After returning to campus from Christmas break, Joy called Angel several days throughout the week until spring break arrived. Then she continued the routine until summer. Joy didn't visit her family outside of breaks, so when summer rolled around she was thankful to spend time at home.

· · · · ·

The first Sunday in June felt like any other Sunday when Joy woke up at 7:30, until she heard Lester and Angel yelling. Lester paced across the bedroom floor. Joy knew it was him because he walked heavier than Angel. Joy couldn't make out what they were saying from her room, so she sat at the bottom of their steps and listened.

"You haven't contributed financially to this household for the entire year," Angel said.

"Well, what about all this money you are spending?"

"What money?"

"This ten thousand dollars you gave to the church. I'm looking at the checkbook now."

"Those are my tithes. What are you talking about?"

"But ten thousand dollars?"

Joy crept to the top of the steps and peeked around the corner, so she could hear better and see what was happening.

"How dare you question the money I give to God. Who are you? Who have you become? You don't work and you are running around on me." Angel paused. "You need to just leave," she demanded as she sat on the edge of their bed, shaking her head.

"Where will I go?" Lester whispered as he leaned into Angel's face.

"That's your problem." Angel stood with her lips tight and sized Lester up with her eyes. She threw her hands up in ultimate surrender.

"Oh, it's my problem, huh? This is my house, too! I'll be damned if you put me out. I ain't going nowhere," he yelled and pressed her against the wall.

"Get your hands off me and get out now," Angel screamed.

"Is this what you call being a submissive wife?" Lester cocked his head slightly and narrowed his eyes.

"Get out! I don't have to submit to a man who has lost his mind," Angel yelled.

"I'll show you crazy if that's what you think I am." Lester picked Angel up and put her over his shoulder.

She struggled to get away, punching him in the head and shoulders to break free. Lester threw Angel on their bed and climbed on top of her. He pinned her between his legs and started choking her.

Angel moaned and fought to get out of Lester's grip. She pounded his head with the last of her energy.

Joy sprinted around the corner when she saw the struggle.

"Get off of my mother," Joy screamed.

Lester jumped off the bed with a crazed look in his eyes.

"Don't you ever put your hands on my mother again," Joy yelled and pushed Lester.

"Did you hear me? Don't ever put your hands on Mom again or I'll call the police."

"Nobody was putting their hands on anybody. You need to calm down before I put my hands on you."

"If you want to put your hands on somebody, I'm right here," Moses yelled, barging into the room.

Moses pushed Lester and then punched him in the face. Lester appeared stunned for a moment, then retaliated. Father and son wrestled on the bedroom floor.

"Enough! Stop fighting!" Angel cried from the bed.

Joy watched in shock.

With much effort, Lester finally pinned Moses, who was nearly as tall as he was, facedown on the floor. After threatening to kill his son if he ever raised his hand to him again, Lester released Moses and stormed down the stairs.

Angel slid to the edge of the bed, put her feet gently on the floor, and stood slowly. Her demeanor was one of defeat. Her eyes whispered shame to Moses and Joy. Without uttering a word, Angel crept into the bathroom.

"Mom, are you okay?" Joy asked, standing behind Angel in the bathroom, rubbing her back. Angel's face was red and puffy, while her neck was covered with small red marks.

Angel's shoulders hunched as she leaned on the bathroom sink and nodded. Angel didn't say a word, but motioned for Joy to leave then closed the bathroom door and started sobbing.

When Joy turned around, Moses was behind her.

"What happened? How did all this start?"

"I was eavesdropping at the bottom of the steps while they were arguing, then I went to the top of the stairs to see what was happening. The yelling escalated and Dad choked Mom."

"Why didn't you call me, so I could help?"

"There was no time. I was already at the top of the stairs and just reacted."

"Get ready for church, now!" Lester yelled up the stairs.

"He's a maniac," Joy whispered to Moses.

"I should've knocked him out when I had the chance, since he wants to put his hands on somebody." Moses balled up his fists and started punching the air like it was Lester's face.

"No offense, Mo, but Dad is strong and crazy. You would have never knocked him out."

"What are we going to do? Should we call the police?" Moses asked.

"Joy and Moses, stop all that talking and get downstairs, now. Get dressed for church. I'm not going to tell you again."

Afraid of what Lester would do next, Joy and Moses did as they were ordered.

While they rode to church in silence, Joy remembered it was communion Sunday. She felt awkward sitting next to Lester during service, while he acted as if nothing had happened. Images of Lester choking Angel arrested Joy's attention the entire day. Moses, on the other hand, cried through most of the service. He tried to hide his tears, but every time Joy looked at him she saw him catch one with his finger. Joy didn't know how to comfort him or make things better. She prayed fervently for the family, and waited for God to answer her prayers.

After church Angel prepared an elaborate meal, which was customary on Sundays. When dinner was ready Angel called Joy and Moses several times before they appeared at the table. Lester was not at home, which relieved Joy since she could not stomach looking at him and eating at the same time.

"Well, you two are quiet." Angel tried to break the deafening silence in the room.

"The choir was exceptional this morning," Joy said as she pushed her potato salad from one side of her plate to the other.

"Were you listening to the same choir I was listening to?" Moses smirked.

"Look you two, I know you're upset by what happened this morning. That was the first time your father ever physically hurt me. It's not right and I want both of you to know that's not acceptable," Angel said, searching for emotion in her children's eyes.

"Should we have called the police?" Moses asked.

"I'm not sure. I was caught off guard like you two were. I was in shock and I didn't know what to do. I don't have all the answers, but I know God does, so I took this to Him in prayer like I do everything else."

"Did you get an answer?" Joy asked.

"What do you mean?" Angel asked.

"Did God give you an answer?"

"Not yet," Angel answered, "but your father did apologize."

"What else would he do? He wants to continue living here," Joy said sarcastically while shaking her head.

"Joy, I know you don't want your father living here anymore, but that is a decision for God to make. He will answer my prayers. I just want you and Moses to know what happened is not okay. I am so sorry, really. I'm sick that you two had to go through this because I know it's changed both of you. It took away some of the childlike innocence that was left. I love you both. Things are going to get better. Please don't worry."

Joy never discussed the choking incident with anyone else but Moses. She tried to bury that image along with the others, but it wouldn't go away. As a result, she was guarded in her own relationships. Joy vowed to never be a victim of love. If this was what for better or worse represented, she didn't ever want to be married.

It was burdensome to live in a home where she did not feel safe. What made it worse was smiling in public when she wanted to scream.

CHAPTER EIGHTEEN

Joy was scheduled to embark on a wonderful journey to South
Africa during winter break of her sophomore year for a two-
week focus trip coordinated by Professor Washington. Joy was
excited about the voyage because she'd never been outside of the
United States, and longed to connect with her African roots. Lester didn't want Joy to go on the trip because he thought it was
too dangerous, but with Angel and Joy tag-teaming Lester, Joy
got her way. She ended up doing a work study to pay for most of
the trip, so the expense wasn't an issue. Angel convinced Lester it
was safe and that Joy would be monitored by chaperones. Lester
never approved of Joy spending time away from home other than
at college, because he was always worried about her safety.

When winter break arrived, Joy was apprehensive about
the fourteen-hour flight, but she knew it was the only way she
would get to South Africa, so she caught a train from downtown
Baltimore to Union Station in D.C., where she met her friend
Cameron, Professor Washington and his father, as well as Hastings music professor Dr. Loshan, who was accompanied by her
husband. They caught a train to New York and from there they
caught a taxi to JFK to board a non-stop flight on South African
Airways to Johannesburg.

The plane was about to land and it could not have come soon
enough for Joy. To her it seemed like they were on the plane
for days. As she gazed out the window, Joy was mesmerized by
the white clouds placed carefully in a sea of blue, blended with

streaks of gray. When the sun peeked through, she knew God was smiling on them.

For years Joy dreamed of going to Africa. It was a destination that once felt out of her reach, although she felt a connection with the continent. Throughout the trip Joy experienced what it felt like to be a visitor in a foreign land. It was not common for blacks and whites to travel as companions in South Africa. In fact, it seemed as if they were the only mixed traveling group in the country. Fifteen people made up the diverse bunch, which was quite a spectacle for the natives of South Africa. Joy quickly realized early on in the trip the one thing she thought would make her feel at home was swallowed up by the "American" that hyphenated part of who she was: African-American.

The entire group crammed into a white traveling van at the airport and headed for a hotel in Pretoria. There were green hills and trees for miles, illuminated by a bright blue sky. The view from the van was like a postcard in motion.

My family and friends could have never imagined the beautiful scenery in South Africa, Joy thought.

She tried to take pictures of every tree and hill during the trip. When they arrived in Pretoria they went straight to the Greta Brae Lodge. It was a nice hotel with all of the accommodations of one in the states. The shiny marble floors and plush sofas and chairs welcomed them for a pleasant stay.

After they unpacked they took a walk to see what was close to their accommodations. In walking distance of their hotel was a KFC and Mercedes Benz dealership, familiar establishments they didn't expect to see in South Africa.

Joy prepared herself early in the morning for the first full day in South Africa. She shared a restroom with four other women and didn't want to be the last one to get ready, so at 6:00 a.m. she rose to beat the bathroom rush. Joy met the group at 7:30 a.m. for breakfast in the lodge restaurant where she received an itinerary from Professor Washington, which was packed with activities.

After breakfast they attended workshops at the Institute for Democracy in South Africa (IDASA) and learned about the current challenges faced by the South African legal system. During the day they also visited the University of South Africa (UNISA), where Dr. Zelda Schwab, an Afrikaner and UNISA history professor, accompanied the group on their tour. She was the personal guide throughout most of their adventures in South Africa. When Joy was introduced to Dr. Schwab she had to look up to her to make eye contact, as she stood at least six feet tall and was very lean. Joy thought she was extremely personable and from the soft lines that were barely visible on her pale skin she appeared to be in her early forties. Her nasally tone and German accent were distinct and made Dr. Schwab's voice unforgettable to Joy.

Joy was amazed UNISA enrolled over one hundred thousand students. Their library was a massive showpiece of six floors, connected by tall, winding silver staircases. After touring the library, they visited the printing press in the basement of the library where UNISA, one of the largest printing productions in the southern hemisphere, printed its books.

Joy treasured the days filled with academic tours, museums, and roundtable discussions, but she learned the most important lessons from the people in South Africa.

Joy realized she took a lot of things for granted at home and vowed to change her attitude into gratitude for being able to live without limitations. Joy gained a renewed sense of freedom, which was acutely felt walking the dismal floors of a prison.

The day began early for Joy, just like the other days in South Africa, because the group had so much to see and very little time, since they were only staying for two weeks. Their voyage began with a ferry ride to Robben Island, four miles off the coast of Capetown. The waters were rough on the thirty-minute ferry; some of the students had to close their eyes so the view of the crashing water against the boat wouldn't add to their nausea. Professor Washington's father moaned for relief as soon as the boat pulled off, complaining he was going to be sick. However, Joy kept her eyes open, taking in the breathtaking views of Capetown and Table Mountain in anticipation of seeing the island she'd heard so much about in her studies.

Joy recognized Robben Island as the place where South Africa's president, Nelson Mandela, was jailed eighteen years for being a political activist, but learned during the visit it was used for many things throughout history including a leper colony, hospital for the mentally and chronically ill, and a training and defense station in World War II. In 1997, the island was turned into a museum. The tour included a round-trip ferry ride to the island from the Nelson Mandela gateway, and an hour-long bus tour of the island followed by a tour of the maximum-security prison.

The group's tour guide, Patrick Manta, a former inmate, spent twenty years in Robben Island, since age nineteen, for speaking against apartheid. He passionately described the injustices that occurred within the prison, including the mental and physical abuse of the prisoners. He attributed forgiveness as the reason he could now work on the island as a tour guide. When Joy walked in the cell where Nelson Mandela was held, she couldn't believe how tiny the quarters were for a man who made such a difference in the world. *What did he think about being confined to this closet with bars?* Joy wondered as she ran her hand along the walls of the cell.

The rest of the afternoon was solemn while Joy and her associates meditated on the island as they journeyed back to their living quarters.

Later that week they traveled to townships on the outskirts of town where black South Africans lived, an area comprised of self-constructed metal houses on dirt roads. Their guide said they had communal outhouses and some running water. Joy never forgot the faces of the people in the townships. She knew the children running after their van would never be afforded the chances children have in the states. Their squalor was inherited by skin color and it was something they could not escape. Seeing the poverty in the townships and meeting the beautiful people warmed and pained Joy's heart simultaneously.

The final destination of their journey was Deo Gloria, which means God's country, a game reserve located forty-five minutes from Johannesburg along the Hartbeespoort Dam at the foot of the Magalies Mountains. Joy thought it was adventurous that they bunked in cabins and ate dinner around a large campfire. The most outdoor activity Joy did in life occurred during summer camp as a child, and that was only a short drive from Baltimore City.

Away from the lights and noise of the city it was easy to hear God speak. Joy heard Him say, "Look at my creation and know that I am God."

At night, Joy and her companions rode along the paths created over time amidst towering trees and high grass. When she listened to the melodious sounds of birds and bugs chirping and buzzing as if they were being led by a symphony director, it prompted Joy to take a deep breath and look up. When she did, Joy was in awe that there were more stars than sky. In that moment, Joy realized she had been deprived of experiencing the beauty of life at its most basic level.

Throughout their travels, Joy began to fall in love with South Africa, but it wasn't a love she could settle in and call home, it was a love only to be visited, like a distant relative.

Joy knew upon her arrival home she would eventually forget some of the things learned and observed in South Africa, but she would never forget the people. The black South Africans were the warmest people she'd ever embraced. They called her "my sister" and didn't hold being American against her. When Joy returned from South Africa she was greeted by Angel, Lester, Moses, and their extended family in the Baltimore train station. Joy was shocked that the first person running to greet her was Gran. It looked like she was sprinting. Joy's family wanted the details of her adventure, so they gathered at a buffet to hear about her experiences during the past two weeks. During dinner, Joy learned everyone was concerned about her safety while away because the news was flooded with fighting and unrest in South Africa.

After dinner, Joy dropped off fourteen rolls of film for development before going home, because she wanted to get started on memorializing her trip in a large photo album.

After a long, hot bath Joy stretched out on her bed, amazed

by how much she'd seen in two weeks. Only one week of winter break left.

Joy slept away the remaining week of her break. The semesters came and went while she tried to keep her grades up, secure an internship for the summer, and maintain an active social life. During the spring semester she joined INROADS, an internship program for college students of color. Through this program she was hired as an intern in the Communications Department for the Decker Box Corporation in Maryland. Joy prepared media kits and met with project managers to fine-tune the graphics for new power tools. She also wrote press releases and observed focus groups where the company tested their latest advertisements. It was her dream internship, because she got paid to work in her field. Joy thought the work was interesting. She loved the responsibility of working a project to completion.

The 1998–1999 academic year ended without any surprises. Joy was a professional packer by then and when Angel, Lester, and Moses picked her up, everything was organized and ready for transport.

By the time summer break arrived, Joy had stopped praying so much for Lester and Angel's marriage and started praying for Angel's well-being. It appeared Angel would never leave Lester no matter what he did, so all Joy could do was pray for her protection.

However, Joy learned during the summer that even Angel had a breaking point.

CHAPTER NINETEEN

*R*ing. "Hello." *Click.*
Ring. "Hello." *Click.*

Ring. "Hello. Look, I'm fed up with the hang-up calls. My father is not here and if he was he wouldn't want to talk to you. So get a life and stop playing on the phone," Joy snapped as she gripped the telephone.

"How do you know he doesn't want to talk to me?"

"Well, he's not here!"

"I'll see when I get there," *she* hissed as she hung up.

"When she gets here? The nerve of that hussy."

Joy turned on the light in her room, tied her headscarf tightly, and slipped into a pair of flip-flops. She paced back and forth in front of the large bay window in the living room and wondered where the center of all this attention was, because Lester obviously wasn't out with the cellular-crazed psycho. Maybe Lester was out with another woman, Joy thought, as she poked her head between the vertical blinds that blocked her view of the street.

While she peered out the window, a woman turned the corner like a witch landing on her broomstick. It was *her.* *She* pulled up across the street and parked. Joy raced to her bedroom and got a piece of paper and a pen. She breathed in deeply and asked the Lord to protect her and give her strength. Then she went outside and walked over to her vehicle.

Joy quickly wrote down her license plate number and tried to get a glimpse of the stalker. It was dark, so she couldn't get a good look, but she didn't see anything that was worth looking at twice. She tried to steady her shaking hands while she wrote. What only took a few seconds seemed like a lifetime. Joy was tempted to open the stalker's door, pull her out of the car, and beat her until some sense seeped into her small brain, but decided not to waste any time on her, and more importantly, get her face scratched up.

After writing the number down she walked fast and hard to the house and closed the door, wondering if the psycho was going to get out of the car and attack her from behind. The woman sat parked in her car for a few more moments, then pulled off.

Ring. "Hello." It was her.

With her chest heaving, Joy picked up and slowly put the phone to her ear, wondering what this woman was going to say.

"What are you going to do? Give my license plate number to the police because I'm sleeping with your father?"

She hung up before Joy could clear her throat to respond. Joy let the phone sit on her ear as she listened in shock to the dial tone. Her heart beat fast. The tears wouldn't stop falling, dripping, racing down her face, meeting at her chin where she finally rubbed the water off with the back of her hand.

Frustrated and furious, Joy paced the length of the living room, wanting to release her emotions on *her*. Joy dialed her number hoping she would answer.

Ring. "What do you want?!"

"I'm a woman. You don't have to call and hang up. We can have a conversation."

"What do you want to talk about?"

"I know my father is having an affair."

"Oh, you do? Is it obvious?"

Joy wanted to slap the sarcasm out of her voice. "We aren't stupid."

"Your mother condones his behavior."

"Don't talk about my mother. She doesn't condone anything. She is a religious woman and she is going to let God deal with him."

"God is the only one who can help him. Your father is sick. He needs psychiatric help. He isn't the man you think he is."

"Then who is he, since you seem to know him so well?"

"Sweetie, you couldn't handle it if I told you."

"So you are tracking down another woman's husband, why? Let me guess. You are in love."

"I've given up so much for him. It seems like he has everything and I have nothing. I don't even know if I want to deal with this anymore."

Conversing about her father's shortcomings with his mistress was a conversation Joy never imagined.

"How long has this been going on?"

"What difference does it make?"

"I want to know."

"Over five years."

"My father had been deceiving us for five years?" Though Joy knew her father was unfaithful, the words pierced her heart when she heard five years because it seemed like it wasn't random flings that kept Lester from them. It was like he created a second life with this woman. *She* had a piece of his heart. Joy gasped for air like someone was holding her hostage under water.

"He needs help, and so do I."

Tears drenched her face as she leaned back in the chair, closed her eyes, and listened to the home-wrecker on the other end. Her voice filled with a rehearsed remorse.

"I have wasted so much of my life fooling around with him. I knew I should have never engaged in a relationship with a man in his situation."

"Situation" was a mild way of putting it—he was a married man with two kids. What did she think she would gain from this situation?

"My mother is a hard worker. She gets up early in the morning and goes to work every day. The least she deserves is a good night's rest."

"I work, too. In fact, I work two jobs and go to school."

"Give me a break. Who cares how many jobs you have or if you're going to school? If you have time to stalk my father and call our house all hours of the night, you must be studying an easy subject," Joy snapped and rolled her neck like the woman could see it through the phone.

"I'm sorry. I didn't mean to harass you or your mom. I wanted to make your father mad. I won't call again."

In the few heart-wrenching minutes of conversation, *she* had confirmed what Joy had known for a while. Her father only cared about himself.

Joy got up from the green chair by the window in the living room feeling drained from the conversation with *her*. She wiped off the phone that was saturated with her tears and put it back on the base, still gripping the piece of paper with the tag number on it, which she later hid in the nightstand.

Joy tossed and turned thinking about what was said on the phone until she heard Lester open the front door at 4:00 a.m.

"So your mistress doesn't just make crank calls, she makes house calls, too?" Joy got in his face to capture his reaction.

Lester looked at Joy like she was crazy, dismissing her with a wave of his hand. He was such a good actor that Joy paused to make sure the confrontation wasn't a dream. She looked outside to see if there were any skid marks from *her* reckless driving and was surprised that *she* was parked across the street.

Joy tried to calculate how many hours had passed since their conversation.

I feel sorry for her. To think that she was so lonely and obsessed she needed to sit in a parked car for hours, waiting for a married man to come home. How could a person be that desperate?

She must have filled Lester in on the events that occurred earlier that night because when Joy confronted him, he brushed her off. It was at that moment Joy decided Lester was going to pay for what he'd done.

The next morning Joy went to Decker Box, feeling like the world was coming to an end. While at work, she rehearsed her speech to Angel. She was going to explain the entire night to her, including the phone calls, writing that woman's tag number down, and the conversation with *her*. Joy couldn't keep any more secrets.

At the end of her shift, Joy drove home completely preoccupied by the conversation she planned to have with Angel. She hoped Angel would be the only person home so they wouldn't be interrupted. When Joy arrived home she smelled something cooking on the grill and knew Angel was preparing dinner. When Joy entered the living room she saw Angel, Lester, and Moses laughing and joking.

He has the nerve to be here joking after what happened last night. He better laugh now because it won't be funny once I tell Mom.

Angel stood between the kitchen and the dining room, leaning over a chair, wearing her black *This Mama Can Cook* apron and holding a long fork in one hand and tongs in the other.

When Lester and Moses went to the hardware store to pick up a knob for the bathroom door, Joy took advantage of the opportunity.

Angel was flipping chicken on the grill when she looked up and saw Joy peering through the screen of the back door.

"What's up?"

"I have something to tell you. It's about Dad."

"Nothing you say about your father will shock me. Tell me what's on your mind."

"Well, some woman kept calling and hanging up on the house phone last night. I was irritated so I used *69 to call her back and left a message." Joy braced herself for Angel's reaction. "She came by the house and parked across the street. I wanted to get something we could give to the police in case she did something crazy, so I went outside and stood behind her car and wrote her tag number down."

"You did what?" Angel grimaced as she nervously twirled the tongs in her hand. "What if this woman had done something to you? She is obviously not in her right mind. Finish the story please."

"Once I wrote the tag number down I went back in the house. A few minutes later she told me she was having an affair with Dad." Joy stood back, waiting for a reaction.

"Your father having an affair is not a surprise to me."

"She said they have been together for five years." Joy shared every detail, so Angel would finally reach the point of total disgust.

"I knew that, too." Angel flipped the chicken on the grill like it was the last supper. "Did you confront your father about it last night?"

"He shrugged me off when I confronted him."

"I'm sure. Joy, you should not have taken matters into your own hands. It grieves me that you had to hear this from that woman. She had no business speaking to you like that, and I wish I would have had the conversation with her instead of you. I will deal with your father. I'm glad you told me. I know you try to keep things from me so I won't worry, but enough is enough." Angel hugged Joy tightly, almost like she was trying to squeeze the weight off of Joy's shoulders.

"Dinner will be ready in a few minutes. I will take care of everything," Angel said, then turned the chicken on the grill.

Joy thought Angel was pretty calm and would brush this incident off like she had done Lester's previous offenses. Joy was eating at the dining room table when Angel opened the front door and left for choir rehearsal. As Angel walked out the front door, Lester and Moses returned from the hardware store. Lester stayed at home even after Angel went to church. Joy wondered what was going to happen when she returned.

When Angel got home it sounded like thunder as she ran up the wooden stairs to their bedroom. As usual Joy tiptoed to the top of the staircase, so she could hear and see what was happening. She also wanted to be there in case Lester got physical, so she could protect Angel.

"Some woman tells our daughter she's sleeping with you and you think that's okay?" Angel leaned over Lester who was sitting on their bed, reading the paper.

"What are you talking about now?" Lester rested his chin on his closed hands.

"I've known you've been cheating on me for years and I'm tired of it," Angel yelled and met Lester's gaze eye to eye.

"Is this my fault? If you would have been a better wife maybe I wouldn't have to get fulfilled elsewhere." Lester stood as if making a valid point.

"You are really delusional. How dare you shift the blame for your affairs on me. You can't be serious. I have been nothing but good to you. I have put up with your unemployment, your temper, your affairs, and your abuse. You have never gone without clean clothes and a hot meal and you have the audacity to talk to me this way?" Angel's arms flailed and her neck rolled. She stood on her tip-toes, straining to reach Lester's face.

"You better watch how you talk to me. I'm a grown man. You don't have to talk to me like that." Lester's voice was loud and his arms were folded, indicating he'd had enough conversation.

"Get out now!" Angel stomped her feet and pointed her index finger toward the stairs.

Lester sat back down on the bed. "Where am I going to go?"

"I don't care where you go. I want you out of here now or I'm going to call the police." Angel used her last bit of energy to stand her ground as perspiration dripped from her brow. "You make me sick. I hope Moses doesn't turn out to be like you. Stay away from the children!" She plopped on the bed, winded from yelling.

"They are my children, too. You can't stop me from seeing my children." He covered his face with his hands and wept.

"I hope *she* and whoever else was worth your family, and your home." Angel pulled Lester's hands away from his face and shook her head. She went into their bathroom and locked the door.

When Lester came downstairs it looked like he was going to take a short walk. He only had a book in his hand and a trench coat thrown over his shoulder.

"I love you guys. Always remember that I love you guys," he announced with a half-smile and hug.

Joy was relieved when he walked out the front door; Moses, on the other hand, cried.

"You are going to miss him?" Joy asked.

"Maybe," Moses answered.

That night Joy slept like a princess. She didn't have to worry about the phone ringing off the hook or the front door creaking open at 4 a.m. Joy was glad she had told Angel about the incident and hoped Lester would never come back home.

The next day Joy went to work refreshed from a good night's sleep. When Joy arrived at home that evening she didn't see Angel's car and figured she was still at work. Since Lester no longer lived with them, Joy would have the house to herself to unwind. When Joy opened the front door she felt steam coming from the bathroom, dashing Joy's hopes of having the house to herself. She figured it was Moses taking a shower before he met one of his many girlfriends to hang out with, but was unpleasantly surprised when the bathroom door opened and Lester appeared out of the steam.

"What are you doing here? You don't live here anymore."

"I don't have any place to go." Lester stood in the living room with a towel wrapped around his waist. "How can you be so mean to your own father?"

"Easy," Joy hissed, folded her arms, and tapped her foot.

Lester stomped up the steps like he belonged in the house. Joy was furious that Lester was back in the house after Angel had thrown him out. She went in her room and shut the door. Joy heard Lester warm a plate of food in the microwave. After about thirty minutes he slammed the front door shut. Joy ran to the window and watched him walk down the street toward the bus stop. Since Angel threw him out, he no longer had access to the family car and had to take public transportation or bum a ride from friends to get around.

When Angel got home Joy told her what had happened. The next day, Angel replaced all the locks and changed the code to the house alarm. She made Moses promise he wouldn't give Lester a key or the code. Angel knew she didn't have to worry about Joy giving Lester anything.

CHAPTER TWENTY

With Lester gone the Noble home was quiet. There were no more prank phone calls or late-night creaking of the front door. There were no more midnight arguments, or mid-morning arguments, or weekend arguments between Lester and Angel. The quiet was deafening for Moses. It was so loud that he tried to drown it out by blasting his music, working as many hours as he could at his part-time job at the mall, or by spending time with one of his female friends.

Moses tried to avoid the place he called home because with all that had happened, it didn't feel like the home he'd grown to love. Lester's departure made the deterioration of the father/son relationship seem final.

Moses noticed that while he drifted further from the family, Joy and Angel seemed to be joined at the hip when Joy was visiting from college. They were like best friends and seemed to comfort each other in a way Moses couldn't identify with as a young man.

Moses applied to a couple of community colleges and one college out of state. He crossed his fingers that he would get into school because his grades weren't the best. When the Christian college he applied to, Freedom University, accepted him, he was thrilled that he could get away from home.

With all of the drama in the house, Angel and Lester didn't take Moses on college tours. When he got accepted, Lester was not around and didn't make the trip to take him to school. Angel,

Joy, and Aunt Pam helped Moses pack and took the ride to Virginia to drop him off at his dorm.

"Well, I guess this is it," Angel said to Moses as she unpacked his last box.

"I guess. Don't worry about me, Mom. I'll be fine," Moses said as he hugged Angel.

"I'll look out for him, Mrs. Noble," Moses's roommate, David, said as he grinned.

David and Moses grew up together in church, and when they found out they were going to be roommates they were relieved. David was six feet tall, light skinned with light brown hair he kept cut low. He had light brown eyes and a wide smile, which welcomed women his way.

"I don't want you guys partying. You are here to get a degree. Do not turn this school into the club. Make sure you two attend Bible study on a regular basis and don't have any girls in this room." Angel peered at Moses and David like she was threatening them.

"We won't, Mom. It will be all about the books and Bible."

Moses laughed and David burst into laughter.

"Books and Bible. That's a good one, Moses," Joy said, shaking her head.

"Moses, do you need anything before we leave?" Angel asked.

"I'm good, Ma. Thanks."

"Well, let's all hold hands and pray before we leave," Angel said. Angel, Aunt Pam, Joy, Moses, and David held hands and formed a circle. Angel led the prayer and asked God not only for traveling grace, but protection for Moses and David as they started their first semester.

After his family's departure, Moses was left wondering what was next for him. He really didn't want to attend college, but wanted to get away from home. He and David managed to meet some freshman females before the day was over and decided to hang out at the campus center.

Later that night they hooked up with a senior and went to a party off campus. They stayed out so late, Moses overslept for his first class. With complete freedom at college, Moses decided to dull his brokenness with women and alcohol. He was good looking like Lester was at his age and women threw themselves at him. Moses emotionally detached himself from relationships and categorized the women in his life as simply friends. He didn't want to put a title on anything so nobody would expect him to be present emotionally.

He thought Lester would have called him to see how he was doing in school, but he never did.

CHAPTER TWENTY-ONE

During Joy's senior year she had a severe case of senioritis, the disorder that causes college seniors to skip class, withdraw from activities, and complete all academic assignments at the last minute. Joy stopped writing for the newspaper, serving on the Student Government Association, and holding an office in The Sistaz. She was burned out. Joy just wanted to relax and spend the year finding the perfect job.

Her senior year was stress-free as far as family was concerned. She no longer worried about what was happening at home because Lester was out of the picture. Even during the holidays Joy didn't miss him.

Their first Christmas without Lester didn't feel awkward for Joy. In fact, she felt merrier. Though Joy was able to get in the holiday spirit, she noticed Angel seemed sad. Joy watched Angel when she was unaware and noticed her moping. Joy wondered if Angel actually missed Lester and wondered why she wasted her emotional energy on him. Joy knew Angel never wanted their family to be broken, because she wouldn't have endured so much pain if it wasn't so important to her. Joy just wanted Angel to let go and enjoy the quiet. Angel's stress level decreased since Lester was out of the house. Moses never really said much about Lester. He put most of his energy into school and work. It seemed Moses was obsessed with keeping a job. The past few holidays, even though Lester was with the family physically, he'd checked out emotionally, so there wasn't too much of an adjustment for anyone.

When Joy awoke on Christmas morning she didn't rush into the living room to see the presents placed under the tree for her. Instead, she stayed in bed and thought about life. After a few minutes of meditating, Angel rushed into Joy's room shouting.

"Merry Christmas! Get up, sleepyhead! Aren't you going to open your presents? It's Christmas morning."

"Aren't you jolly this morning," Joy teased as she sat up.

Joy went into the living room expecting one or two gifts, but was shocked when the entire room was filled with beautifully wrapped boxes. While Joy started opening her gifts, Angel went into Moses's room and started bouncing on his bed so he would get up, too. Joy thought the role reversal was hysterical. Now Angel was the one excited about opening gifts while Joy and Moses just wanted to sleep.

Joy was concerned the bountiful Christmas gifts were Angel's attempt to make up for Lester's disappearing act. If that was the purpose behind all the presents, Joy thought Angel was wasting her time and money.

Joy often asked Angel a lot of hypothetical questions about taking Lester back. It was her strategy to gauge Lester's chances of ruining their lives again. Angel never gave a definite answer, and her responses often puzzled Joy, but after Angel talked in circles for a few moments, she would always end their conversation the same way: "God is in control of this situation. God can change your father. Don't you believe God can do anything?"

· · · · ·

During the spring semester Joy spent her free time looking for jobs. She applied to fifty jobs in December before the end of the fall semester. When she didn't receive any responses to her applications, Joy started calling contacts to see if they knew of any openings in the mass communications field. One of her contacts led to a phone interview with a woman who worked for the Charm City newspaper, Muriel.

Joy met Muriel through the manager of the Baltimore INROADS office. Instead of concentrating on helping Joy get a job at the Charm City paper, all Muriel discussed was the master's program at Orange University. Joy didn't want to offend her, so she waited quietly until Muriel finished her pitch. Joy did not want to attend graduate school immediately, because she was in a lot of debt and wanted to work full-time. However, after Muriel's convincing argument, Joy agreed to take the Graduate Record Examination (GRE) and consider applying for graduate school. What she really wanted was for Muriel to get her an interview with someone at the Charm City paper. Muriel promised to give Joy a telephone interview in a couple of weeks.

Joy was disappointed with her GRE results and didn't think they were good enough to get accepted into a graduate program, but decided to step out on faith and apply. She didn't make that life-changing decision until late January, while the application deadline was in February. Joy asked two of her professors for recommendations and she wrote a passionate essay about her aspirations and the opportunities she'd been afforded through education. She completed and mailed the application just a few days before the deadline. Joy knew it would be a miracle if she was accepted.

After she submitted the application, Joy didn't think about it again until she received a package in the mail from Orange University in April. Joy stared at the large envelope for a few minutes before she opened it. As she tore it open, butterflies filled her belly as beads of sweat formed on her brow. Taking deep breaths to calm down, Joy was surprised at how her nerves quickly spiraled out of control. She didn't understand why she was nervous because she didn't want to go to graduate school, but she realized with no job offers her options were limited. Joy hadn't received one response to any of the job applications she mailed. Despite her shaking hands, Joy managed to unravel the letter to read the response to her application.

Joy Noble, we are pleased to inform you that you were selected for our graduate program . . .

She read the rest of the letter, jumping up and down on her

bed. Joy was so loud her roommate ran over to see what the fuss was about.

"Are you all right? What is going on?"

"I was accepted to Orange University. I'll be getting my master's in journalism."

"You go, girl. I am so proud of you, Joy. I told you graduate school was the way to go."

"What is Marley going to say about you going away to school again? Every chance he gets he's visiting you here. That is, when you guys are 'together,'" Kayla said as she made air quotes with her skinny fingers and rolled her eyes.

"He'll survive. I think I'm going to break it off with him since I'm moving."

"Joy, you are cold. I mean, how many times are you going to break his poor heart?"

"I have to call my mom and tell her the good news."

Joy grabbed the phone and dialed home, while jumping up and down and dancing around her room.

"Hello."

"Hi, Mom," Joy yelled.

"Hi, what's up?"

"Are you sitting down? I have something to tell you."

"What's wrong?" Angel whispered like she was bracing herself for the worst news ever.

"Nothing is wrong, I got some great news. I was accepted into graduate school," Joy screamed.

Angel screamed so loud Joy had to hold the phone away from her ear.

"Praise the Lord. I told you graduate school was best for you. God is good. Read me the letter. Read me the letter."

Joy read the letter line by line until she reached the end, then she read it to Angel again slowly at her request. With all the excitement about getting into Orange's program, Joy hadn't read the remainder of the information attached to the acceptance letter.

Orange University's graduate journalism program was a

one-year intensive course, and classes started the last week of June. Joy couldn't believe how quickly she had to move to a new place and start school again. Joy had never been to upstate New York before, but that would be her new home, at least for a year.

The end of the semester came faster than Joy expected. Before she knew it, Joy was getting fitted for her cap and gown. Angel, being the proud mom, sent Joy's graduation picture and announcement to the entire world, or so it seemed. With the invitations sent out, the dinner plans confirmed, and Joy's final grades posted, all she had to do was walk across the stage without falling.

During the days leading up to graduation, Joy reflected on her life. She thought about the years she'd spent at Hastings, the friends she'd made and the friends she'd lost. She thought about the parties, classes, trips, activities, and people that shaped her college experience. Joy learned as much about life outside of the classroom as she did inside the classroom. The most important lesson learned at Hastings was she could accomplish anything if she trusted God and took one step forward.

CHAPTER TWENTY-TWO

The Saturday before graduation was busy. Joy had to finish packing and pick up her cap and gown. Angel and Moses came up the weekend prior and packed all Joy's belongings except for her clothes, which she would transport in her car.

Later that night Joy's friends stopped by her apartment to reminisce over the good times they'd shared. They could not believe the class of 2001 would walk across the stage tomorrow and go their separate ways. When they left it was almost midnight, but Joy was determined to look great on her big day. She washed and rolled her tresses so her hair would bounce when she walked across the stage. Marley promised Joy he was going to see her walk across the stage and she wanted to look nice for him. They were on again and Joy was looking forward to seeing him. Throughout undergrad, Joy dated Marley on and off, just like in high school. The months leading up to graduation, Marley and Joy managed to stay in a relationship. He'd sent a dozen roses to Joy's apartment every week for the past month and managed to work marriage into all of their conversations.

When Joy and Marley got together this last time, Joy stopped seeing her on-again/off-again friends she lost interest in after only a couple dates.

Hastings's graduation fell on Mother's Day. It was a pleasantly sunny Sunday morning and Joy felt good. She put on a slinky black dress and black high-heeled sandals that highlighted her long brown legs. Joy styled her hair to perfection, wearing it down with a little bounce from the curls, just the way she liked it. A touch of makeup and a few sprays of body mist and Joy was ready for the momentous occasion.

While Joy prepared to greet her family as they arrived that morning, her phone rang. She figured it was someone calling for directions to the ceremony.

"Hello."

"Hi, beautiful. You excited?" Marley asked.

"Hey, babe! Of course I'm excited! It's not every day I graduate from college." Joy laughed.

"Well, I'm going to have to meet you after the graduation ceremony because I'm running a little late. Is that okay?"

"That's fine. I'll see you in a little while."

"Okay, Ms. Noble, see you soon. I love you."

Joy looked at the phone and paused, wondering why Marley was being so mushy, but she shrugged it off and decided not to question his sentiment.

"Love you, too. See ya later. Bye."

Joy's family arrived at her apartment at 10:30 that morning. Only half of them caravanned to Pennsylvania for the graduation because Joy's cousin Kira was graduating on the same day, from a prestigious university down south. The family picked names out of a hat to decide who would attend Joy's graduation and who would attend Kira's. That caused a little tension because both of them wanted Gran to see them walk across the stage. When they drew names, Gran picked Joy's name out of the hat. Joy was ecstatic Gran would be at her graduation, but was saddened that the entire family would not see her walk across the stage.

Joy brought her family to campus early to make sure they got seats with a favorable view of the ceremony. Moses was in charge of protecting their row of seats and videotaping the day so the family who went to Kira's graduation could feel like they participated in Joy's big day, too. While Joy was preparing to line up for the processional, she spotted her Uncle Fence, Aunt Georgette, and their daughter, Georgetta, grabbing their seats in the row Moses saved for the family. When Joy greeted them and thanked them for coming, they said they wouldn't have missed this day for anything in the world. Joy was so touched by the overwhelming support of her family and friends she started to cry, but she quickly got it together so her makeup wouldn't get messed up.

Shortly after Uncle Fence and his family arrived, Joy's friends from home, Wanda, La, and Renee walked over to congratulate her. La brought her daughter, Destiny. Joy was so happy to see them, knowing not too many people would drive two-and-a-half hours on Mother's Day to see a friend graduate. Joy looked around one last time for Lester. She didn't see him.

The graduation ceremony took place outside on the campus lawn between two class buildings. The processional line formed and Lester still hadn't arrived. On the way to her designated spot in line, Joy stopped several times to pose for pictures.

When "Pomp and Circumstance" started playing, the graduates processed in a single-file line from the campus lawn to their seats. This was the beginning of a new world for these students. As Joy walked, she still didn't see Lester. She decided not to dwell on his absence and let him ruin her moment.

Joy daydreamed throughout the entire ceremony. When she came out of her daze, the Dean of Student Affairs, Dr. Richard Waters, started calling names. Joy cheered and clapped for her classmates like she personally knew every student.

When her row lined up at the stage, Joy felt butterflies fluttering around in her stomach. Finally, Joy Marie Noble was called. Joy felt like she was dreaming. Walking across the stage, shaking the university president's hand, and accepting her degree was a blur. As she stepped off the stage Joy posed for more pictures.

I made it across the stage without falling; now I can relax and enjoy this day.

Photos were snapped and people cheered as she continued walking to her seat. That's when Lester grabbed Joy and kissed her on the cheek. Then he presented her with a bouquet of flowers. Joy was shocked when she saw Lester because she almost didn't recognize him. Lester was very thin, his skin darker than usual and his hair completely white. Joy held back the tears trapped in

155

her emotions that overwhelmed her when embraced by Lester. Though she resented him, she was happy he made it to her graduation. It meant he cared. Lester stood wearing dark sunglasses and a suit that almost swallowed his small frame. Joy had not seen Lester in two years and couldn't help but stare in pity wondering why he looked so frail, almost ill. But she couldn't ponder his appearance too long because Angel kindly moved Lester out of the way so she could hug Joy and present her with two dozen long-stemmed roses.

Behind Angel stood Marley, grinning from ear to ear, with a huge bouquet of flowers, dressed in a suit and tie.

"Congratulations, baby! I'm so proud of you."

As Joy accepted the bouquet from Marley, he got down on one knee and pulled a small black felt box out of his inside jacket pocket.

"I've loved you since we were in high school. I can't imagine my life without you. Joy Marie Noble, will you do me the honor of being my bride?"

It seemed like everything stopped and the entire audience was looking at Joy's mouth, waiting for an answer. Angel, Lester, the rest of the family, and Joy's friends were shocked by Marley's proposal.

Joy wanted to run and hide behind the stage, but didn't want to make a bigger scene.

"Yes. Yes, I'll marry you."

Marley stood up and kissed Joy. He lifted her a few inches off the ground like he wanted to carry her away.

The audience cheered with excitement at Joy's response.

"Well, it looks like one of our students is already working on her MRS degree." Dr. Richard Waters laughed before he started calling the rest of the names.

Joy took her seat, worried about how she was going to break the news to Marley after the ceremony. At the end of the program the graduates exited to the student center. The entire campus was a zoo. Joy's friends from home found her walking from the student center.

"Congratulations," they yelled.

"So you graduated and now you're planning a wedding?" La asked.

"You know I'm not marrying Marley. I just said yes, so he wouldn't be embarrassed in front of all those people."

"I didn't think you would marry him, but you never know what people do after college." La smiled. "Well, Marley is looking for you, so be strong and be direct."

"Of course. Thanks for coming, girls. I appreciate it. I'll see you at dinner, right?" Joy asked.

"Yeah, we'll be there," they chimed.

"Oh, a heads-up, your father asked your mother for a kiss by the stage and your mother said, 'I don't think so,'" Wanda said. "Then we left."

No sooner had Wanda finished her comment, Lester strolled up.

"Congratulations, baby." Lester beamed. "La, would you mind taking a picture of us?"

"So I guess you will be packing to leave for Orange University?" Wanda asked.

"You're going to get your master's?" Lester asked. "What are you going to get your master's in?"

"Journalism." Joy sighed while shaking her head, annoyed Lester didn't have a clue about anything.

Angel found them moments later on the walkway. Apparently she and Gran were waiting for Joy by the graduation stage.

"Joy, what is this getting married about? I didn't even know you and Marley were dating again," Angel said.

"I'm not marrying Marley, Mom. I just said yes so he wouldn't look like a fool in front of everyone."

"Joy, you should have never let it go this far. That poor boy. You can't hurt people like this, honey; it's not right."

"How was I supposed to know he was going to propose? He didn't mention it to me. He never asked me about a ring or anything. I hadn't even told him I was going to graduate school yet."

"Okay, calm down, he's walking this way. Please handle this

now and don't cause a scene," Angel said as she ducked out of the way.

"Hey, love, I've been looking all over for you. Let me see that rock on your finger." Marley smiled as he grabbed Joy's left hand.

"Can I talk to you for a minute in private?" Joy pulled Marley away from the main walkway close to a tree for a little privacy on the crowded campus.

"Sure. What's wrong, babe?" Marley calmly asked as he scratched his head.

"Marley, I don't want to marry you."

"What!" Marley yelled.

"Joy, you okay?" Lester asked from a few steps away.

"I'm fine, Dad," Joy yelled back to Lester.

"Please calm down and hear me out. I care about you, but I'm not in love with you. I said yes because you made such a scene at the ceremony, I didn't want to make things worse by saying no. I'm sorry. I hope you will forgive me one day." Joy slid off the two-carat ring Marley had slid on less than an hour before and placed it in his hand.

"Can I have a hug?" Joy asked.

"No, you can't. I'm blown away that you still have commitment issues after all these years. When are you going to grow up? Stop acting like a little girl, Joy, and join me in the real world. I'm tired of your relationship issues."

"Look, I was trying to be nice to you, but you've got it all wrong. First of all, I am not a little girl. I'm a grown woman. A grown woman who graduated from college, a grown woman who is enrolled in graduate school and starting this summer, a grown woman who has worked hard to buy the things I want, like my own car. The list goes on about what this grown woman has done. I'm not marrying you because I'm not in love with you. I don't have relationship issues. I just don't want you." Joy stood on her tiptoes so she could get as close to Marley's face as possible.

"Okay. And you have the nerve to go to graduate school and not tell me."

"See, this is what you aren't understanding. We aren't together, we will never get married, and this is the end of our on-again/off-again thing we've had since high school. I wish you the best."

"Fine, Joy! You will never meet a man that will treat you as good as I have. I'm walking away and I'm not coming back."

"Bye, Marley."

As Marley walked away, Angel stood behind Joy and rubbed her back.

"Are you okay?" Angel asked.

"I'm fine, Mom. Just a little embarrassed from the scene. I hope everyone enjoyed this episode from the *Young, Black, and the Restless*." Joy smiled and hugged Angel.

Lester gave Joy a gift bag and told her he wouldn't make the dinner party. Joy knew she wouldn't see him again anytime soon. They made dinner reservations for 4:00 at BJ's Steak and Rib House. Afterward, everyone gathered at Joy's apartment where she opened her gifts, while the family ate cake and drank coffee for a few hours. Later that night they drove home and Joy spent one last night in her apartment. Kayla and Joy chatted the rest of the night about how much fun they had over the past few years.

"School won't be the same without you, Joy. You truly left your mark at Hastings. I'm going to miss you," Kayla said as she started to cry.

Joy sighed in relief that she had finished this chapter of her life, and was ready to turn the page.

The next morning Joy packed her little red car and prepared to drive home from Pennsylvania one last time. The car was filled with clothes and other small items. Joy said her goodbyes to Kayla and headed south to Baltimore. She was thankful for the quiet car ride alone. Joy used that time to think about her life and what she wanted to do next. She thought about all the horrible things Marley said to her at graduation and wondered if he had any valid points. But Joy knew even if she had commitment issues, that had nothing to do with not wanting to marry Marley. Joy wasn't sure where marriage would fall in the picture of her life, but she was happy it wasn't any time soon.

Joy wouldn't have much time to figure anything out before she started classes. She only had five weeks at home for summer vacation, since the graduate program started the last week of June.

The night before she left for Orange University, Joy's friends came over to spend some time with her. They watched movies and ate Chinese food. Joy was packing the rest of her things and trying to spend time with them at the same time. As usual, Joy waited until the last moment to pack. To get everything done, she would take turns watching a movie with the girls in the basement and running to her room to help Angel pack the rest of her belongings. Angel and Joy were sitting on the floor in her room surrounded by clothes when her friends came in to see the packing progress.

"Look at all this stuff. You are going to be packing all night," Wanda said.

"Joy has to make sure she looks good when she goes to Orange University. She might meet a good man in New York," La instigated.

"Yeah, she might give some of us hope," Renee said.

"Yeah, right. I'm not looking for any man. Good men don't exist," Joy said.

"I told Joy I think the Lord is going to bless her with the man she is going to marry in New York," Angel said.

"I'm going to New York to do my work and get my master's. I'm not looking for a husband, Mom."

"You are going to meet your future husband in New York. I am sure of it," Angel said.

There was no sense in arguing with Angel about what the Lord was going to do for Joy in New York, so Joy just let her talk. They didn't finish packing until 2:00 a.m. At 6:00 a.m., Angel and Joy loaded the rental truck, along with Joy's car, and drove to Syracuse, New York.

CHAPTER TWENTY-THREE

Joy prayed during the entire drive to Orange University that her little red car would not break down. She needed the car to last at least one more year. As she drove north, Joy took in the mountains and the sun shining as a blessing for the journey. The scenery reminded her of Pennsylvania, but without the confederate flags.

Joy drove for two-and-a-half hours before they stopped at a gas station, stretched their legs, and bought snacks for the rest of the road trip. Aunt Pam, who accompanied Angel and Joy on the trip, offered to drive the rest of the way to Orange University, and Joy gladly accepted. Aunt Diane also made the trek to upstate New York, keeping Angel company in the rental truck.

When they reached the campus after a five-hour drive, Joy pulled out her to-do list. The first task was to pick up Joy's apartment keys. She'd already received her class schedule for the summer, but was eager to see her apartment. The campus was so much larger than Hastings's that the university provided shuttle busses for students to get around. She observed as soon as she arrived at the university she was not one of a few brown faces on campus, but one of many compared to undergraduate. The only thing Joy wished was similar to Hastings was the scenery. It wasn't a neatly manicured campus with tons of trees and dorms perfectly placed along quiet streets, but it appeared to be more like a disconnected massive city where you could only find your way to class with a map.

Angel and her sisters waited outside while Joy ventured into the student center to pick up her keys. When she entered the building she noticed a young black guy who was also picking up his apartment keys. Joy knew she looked terrible, but that didn't discourage her from responding when he introduced himself.

"Hi, how are you?" the young man said. "My name is Shawn."

"I'm fine. Well, maybe not today." Joy grinned as she tightened her ponytail to tame her hair. "My name is Joy."

"Oh, you are still fine, Ms. Joy. Is that like the song 'Joy Unspeakable Joy'?" He laughed heartily.

Joy thought Shawn looked like a football player. He was about five-foot nine-inches tall and he was solid. He wasn't big, but he was in shape. His skin was smooth, a medium brown complexion, like a milk-chocolate candy. The only facial hair he could rub while talking to Joy was a little bit of fuzz on the point of his chin. His eyes were round and dark brown. He wasn't Joy's type, as she typically liked very tall guys. She and Shawn were almost the same height and Joy cringed at the thought of wearing high heels and being taller than him, even if only for a little while. Joy stopped thinking about Shawn's physical shortcomings and returned to the conversation.

"I'm glad you find your own jokes funny. That was cute. So you know something about gospel music?"

"I was raised in church, so I know a lot of gospel music. I also study the Bible. What about you? With a name like Joy, you probably have a minister for a father." He smiled and chuckled.

"I was also raised in church, and your minister joke actually hits home. Are you in the graduate program?"

"Yes, I'm in the advertising program. What about you?"

"I'm in the journalism program. It looks like we'll have some courses together." Joy smirked and tried not to beam with excitement that they would see each other again.

"That will work. I'm going to need a study partner." Shawn put his hands in his shorts pockets and shrugged.

"You need a study partner already. I bet. Where are you from?" Joy thought his flirting was cute and though he didn't seem like her type physically, he made her laugh and she liked that a lot.

"I'm from California. What about you, Joy? What is your last name?"

"I thought I traveled a distance. You traveled across the map. I'm from Baltimore, and the last name is Noble."

"Yeah, I'm a long way from home, but that's cool. My last name is Taylor, Ms. Noble."

Joy noticed how plump Shawn's lips were when he talked.

"Well, I have my keys, so I need to move into my place. I'll see you around, Shawn. It was nice meeting you." Joy smiled as she walked toward the door.

"Nice meeting you, too. I'm sure we'll be bumping into each other a lot. Don't forget about the Shawn Taylor study program." Shawn winked and threw his hands up.

Shawn waved to Joy from across the walkway as she and her family moved her belongings in. Since Shawn lived in the building across from Joy's, they would be seeing more of each other.

By the time Shawn offered to help Joy move in, the ladies had already finished unloading everything.

"Hey, Joy, I'm sorry I missed out on helping you move in, but I still want to spend time with you. Would you like to watch a movie at my place tonight?" Shawn asked, then eagerly awaited Joy's answer.

"Sure, that would be cool. I'll stop by when my family leaves," Joy said, trying not to smile.

He seemed cool, but Joy hoped he wasn't trying to get with her because she was there for work, not to date. She was glad she met somebody to hang out with, so there would be at least one familiar face when classes started.

Later that evening, Joy stopped by Shawn's apartment. His roommate, John, also from California, opened the door. Shawn said John lived in a rich area. Joy didn't know anything about California, so she took his word for it.

"How are you? I'm John. You must be Joy. Shawn said you would be stopping by. I'll get him for you."

"Thanks, nice to meet you, John," Joy said as she entered the apartment and looked around.

It was a typical bachelor's pad. Video games were plugged into the television and no décor. Not one picture hung on the white walls. They'd just moved in and maybe they'd fix up the place later, Joy thought, but doubted.

"Hey, Joy." Shawn smiled as he entered the living room. "Thanks for coming over. You want to watch a movie? I'm just eating dinner in my room."

"Sounds good. What movie do you have?" Joy asked as she followed Shawn to his room. Normally, she wouldn't have felt so comfortable with someone she just met, but something about Shawn's eyes made Joy feel like she could trust him.

Shawn's apartment was identical to Joy's. Dark blue carpet covered all the floors except the kitchen and bathroom, while all the walls were a shade of white that had lost its luster.

"The movie choice for tonight is *Love Jones*," Shawn said as he searched for Joy's approval of his selection.

"One of my favorite movies! How did you know?" Joy laughed as she sat on the edge of Shawn's neatly made bed.

"It seems like it's every young woman's favorite movie," Shawn said.

While Shawn set up his laptop to play the movie, Joy looked around his room and noticed it was neat for a guy. He had a lot of CDs and DVDs stacked up in racks on the floor. The room was small, but a good size for college housing.

They sat on Shawn's twin bed and watched the movie while Shawn ate dinner. Joy was shocked by the small amount of food on his plate. He had two small chicken strips, and no more than two scoops of rice and mixed vegetables on his plate.

"Is that all you are going to eat?" Joy asked.

"Yeah," Shawn said with an attitude. "I don't eat a whole lot most of the time and I'm particular about what I eat, no red meat and no pork."

"Really! A guy who eats healthy. You are strange." Joy laughed.

"Laugh now, but I'm healthy." Shawn looked at Joy and smirked like he'd made his point.

They got more than halfway through the movie when Joy started nodding.

"I'm going to go back to my place. I'm tired."

"Oh okay, I understand. Maybe we'll finish watching it another time," Shawn said as he got up to walk Joy out of his room and to the front door.

"Thanks again for the invite. Sorry I wasn't the best company."

"No problem. It's been a long day for you with moving in and all. You want to meet here on Monday, so we can catch the shuttle to class together?" Shawn asked.

"Sure, I'd like that. See you later," Joy said as she headed back to her apartment.

To Joy, the first day of graduate school was like the first day of class at any other academic institution. It was filled with introductions and agendas. Joy's classmates were extremely diverse in their backgrounds. Some had left full-time careers, some had just finished undergraduate like Joy, some were married with children, and some were international students. One thing that stood out to Joy was the female-to-male ratio in their program. The women definitely outnumbered the men, eight to one.

The summer program combined all of the advertising, journalism, and graphic design students in the same courses to prepare them for the fall semester. On Monday, Tuesday, and Wednesday mornings, they took a crash course in journalism, while on Thursday and Friday mornings they went to a graphic design course, and attended lab in the afternoon. The rest of the intense curriculum included an interactive segment of researching and interviewing for articles due weekly.

Shawn and Joy decided to sit together in class. Actually, the two of them ended up doing everything together. They applied for student loans together, caught the bus together, studied together, and ate most of their meals together. Joy found Shawn easy to talk to and he made her laugh. Not that cute giggle when you are trying to impress someone, but that hearty laughter that comes from your belly and tickles your throat when it comes out. They shared their dreams and fears with each other. Like Joy, Shawn did not have a good relationship with his father. He was working on it and said he was making some progress with his dad and encouraged Joy to start the process of forgiving Lester.

Joy and Shawn kept each other company without the drama of being a couple. Joy liked cooking and didn't mind having Shawn over for dinner every night. Especially since she cooked portions large enough for ten, that way the food wouldn't go to waste. Since Shawn chipped in for groceries and insisted on cleaning the kitchen after Joy cooked dinner, for Joy it was the perfect relationship.

Even though they weren't seeing each other romantically, all of their peers thought otherwise. The professors even called them a couple. Joy never focused on Shawn's appearance until she overheard some of her classmates discussing his good looks, which made her look at him more intently. *He is fine,* Joy thought. As she became more attracted to Shawn, hearing other women talk about him made her a little jealous.

Every weekday after class they rode home together and parted for about thirty minutes before Shawn came over for dinner. They studied at Joy's apartment and hung out until they got on each other's nerves.

"Okay, it's time for you to leave, Shawn." Joy pointed her index finger at her front door and pursed her lips like she meant business.

"What are you kicking me out for now?" Shawn shook his head like Joy was being ridiculous.

"Maybe it's because you keep repeating everything I say, or try to take over my computer to check email when I have an assignment to complete, or just because I'm tired of hearing you crack jokes that aren't funny." Joy rolled her eyes and opened the front door.

"You don't have to kick me out, I'll leave. You know you're going to miss me when I'm gone." Shawn smiled as he exited.

"Doubt it," Joy said as she closed the door behind him.

"What are you up to?" Joy called Shawn later that evening.

"Playing video games, thinking about how mean you are to me." Shawn laughed as he paused the game.

"Whatever. Are you going to meet me so we can walk to the bus stop tomorrow morning?" Joy asked.

"Don't we always walk to the bus stop? Tomorrow won't be any different. Don't eat all the apple pie you made tonight so I can have some. See you tomorrow."

"Okay, see you tomorrow." Joy sighed as she hung up the phone. She noticed how she started missing Shawn when they weren't together, though she wasn't sure why.

Joy met Shawn at his apartment to catch the shuttle to campus for the summer farewell luncheon. Joy was relieved that she made it through the brutal summer curriculum and could take a break for a week. She was so caught up in the excitement of finishing the semester that she almost overlooked the silence as they traveled that afternoon.

"What's wrong with you?" Joy asked as she pushed Shawn lightly on his shoulder.

"Nothing. What are you talking about now?" Shawn said quietly.

"Why are you so quiet today? You've barely said anything since we caught the shuttle to campus. Normally I can't get a word in when we walk."

"Nothing."

"I don't believe you. We've been walking to class together the entire semester and this is the first time you're speechless. Give it up, Shawn. Something is going on." Joy looked in his eyes to see if she could magically read his pupils for an answer.

"I'm good. Is something on your mind?" Shawn replied.

"No, I'm fine. Just hungry."

"Why doesn't that surprise me?"

"Speaking of being hungry. Not only are you quiet, but you are walking slower than usual. Pick up the pace, short stuff!" Joy yelled like she was running a boot camp.

Joy started speed-walking ahead of Shawn, but would glance back to see how far he was trailing behind.

Sometimes Joy caught Shawn staring at her, as he trailed a few steps behind her stride. When she caught him, he would always play it off like he was looking somewhere else. Joy thought he was looking at her butt, though she decided not to call him out since he seemed to be in some sort of funk.

When Shawn and Joy arrived at the luncheon late, their classmates made jokes that they looked like they were two lovebirds coming from an afternoon stroll. That wasn't the case, but only Joy and Shawn were convinced of that because their peers already tagged them as an old married couple. As usual, Joy and Shawn laughed it off and let them know they were just friends, nothing more.

At the end of the luncheon, Joy asked a few classmates to stop by her apartment for one last gathering before they parted for the summer. They had a week off before fall semester began and a lot of people were going home. It was one of the few opportunities they had to hang out with no pending assignments.

"Thanks for having us over, Joy. You're always hosting a gathering and you do it so well," one of her classmates said as the others nodded in agreement.

"Don't mention it; you know I love to entertain. I get it from my mom." She smiled as she pulled out some menus to Chinese food delivery places in the area.

They planned to order Chinese food, watch a few movies, and chat at Joy's place for the evening. After a few hours of chatting and dining, Shawn pulled Joy aside in the kitchen.

"I'm going to slip out for a few minutes and bake some cookies," Shawn said.

"Why do you have the sudden urge to bake cookies?" Joy looked at Shawn like he was crazy.

"I need to get rid of that huge bucket of cookie dough I bought a few weeks ago and I thought now would be a good time since we're hanging out." Shawn looked at Joy like she should have known that.

"Okay, whatever. Don't hurt yourself. We both know you don't know the first thing about baking nor turning on an oven." Joy snickered.

"You think you're such a comedian. I'll be back in a few minutes. Don't miss me too much." Shawn smiled.

While Shawn baked, Joy cleaned up the kitchen and took the trash to the dumpster, which was past Shawn's apartment.

"What's up, Betty Crocker?" Joy teased as she yelled through Shawn's screen door.

"I got your Betty Crocker." Shawn smiled and pulled the chocolate chip cookies out of the oven.

"I just stopped in to see if the cookies were ready." Joy peeked over his shoulder to see if he managed to mess up the cookies.

"They're done. I just have to put them on a plate. Wait for me."

Shawn put the cookies on a plate and covered them with Saran Wrap. Joy was walking toward the front door when Shawn grabbed her waist from behind and kissed her on the neck.

Joy froze.

Caught off guard and unsure how to respond, Joy slowly turned around and faced Shawn. Their eyes locked and she wondered if he was looking for the same thing she was. Would they be in each other's future? Instead of speaking, she kissed him until their breaths were intertwined.

His lips are so soft I could kiss him all night, Joy thought.

They stopped kissing and paused in the awkward silence of crossing the friendship line.

"So," Shawn said as he caressed Joy's cheek.

"So what does this mean?" Joy whispered as she looked into Shawn's eyes.

"This means I like you, and I've liked you for a while, but I didn't know if you felt the same way," Shawn said.

"I wasn't sure how I felt. I know I miss you when you're not around and I've thought about what it would be like if we kissed, but I haven't thought past that. And since we're here, I don't know what's next." Joy leaned her head on Shawn's shoulder.

"Well, I hope more kissing is what's next." Shawn smiled. "Seriously, I hope transforming our friendship into a great romantic relationship is next, if that's what you want."

Joy felt warm. It was like the sun was shining on her face as she pulled away from Shawn's shoulder and looked at him.

"Why don't we take these chocolate chip cookies back to my apartment and talk about us when my company leaves?" Joy said softly as she hugged Shawn.

"That sounds like a plan. Let's go." Shawn grabbed the plate of cookies and hugged Joy from behind as they left his apartment.

Back at Joy's apartment, after watching three movies, everyone finally decided to leave. That was everyone except Shawn. He used Joy's computer to check his email, while Joy went to the bathroom to freshen up. None of the apartments were air conditioned, so she had to depend on a fan to keep her cool during the hot days and muggy nights.

When she came out of the bathroom, the lights were turned off in the living room and in the kitchen. Shawn was sitting on the sofa, watching television.

He moves fast when he wants to, Joy thought.

Joy felt a little awkward walking over to the sofa, since there was nothing preventing them from being close to each other and that worried her, not wanting to take things too far. She sat next to Shawn on the sofa, but avoided his eyes. Joy felt comfortable with Shawn, but they were in new territory.

Shawn took her hand and pulled Joy even closer to him. Joy sat on his lap while he gently put his massive arms around her shoulders.

"I care about you. I've wanted to tell you for weeks now," Shawn said as he kissed Joy on the cheek.

"I've been developing feelings for you, too, but I don't think a relationship is a good idea," Joy said as she thought about her failed relationship with Marley and the proposal gone wrong at graduation. She remembered at one time they were great friends, and now they don't speak.

"Why is it a bad idea if we both have feelings for each other?" Shawn rested his chin on Joy's shoulder.

"Shawn, I love spending time with you and I like you, but I don't want to be in a relationship right now." Joy got up from sitting on Shawn's lap and sat next to him on the sofa.

"Why don't you want to be in a relationship? Please don't tell me I got to pay for what the last brother did." Shawn shook his head and prepared for Joy's response like he'd heard it all before.

"No, you aren't paying for any of my exes; they are old news. I just want to focus on school without any distractions. Plus, you are my friend and if this doesn't work, I'll lose one of the coolest, bestest, funniest guy friends I've ever had." Joy hoped her grin would convince Shawn to see it her way.

"Well, if we're not going to be together, you gonna have to mess your hair up and start wearing some baggy jeans or something, because I can't stop thinking about you."

"I'll see what I can do." Joy laughed. "So are we cool?"

"We're cool for now, but I don't give up easily, Ms. Noble. Before it's all over your last name will be Taylor. Good night." Shawn hugged Joy tightly and kissed her on the cheek then left.

The next morning Joy rushed through breakfast in order to catch a ride to Maryland with a friend for the week-long break. When she heard the car horn, she grabbed her bags and opened the door to find a long-stemmed rose and an envelope addressed to *My Friend* neatly placed between the front and screen door. She blushed and picked up the rose, then placed the letter in her purse to read later. While Joy got into her friend's car, she noticed Shawn peeking through the curtain in his kitchen window, but acted like she didn't see him.

CHAPTER TWENTY-FOUR

Joy waited until she arrived at home for her semester break before she opened the envelope. She sat on the edge of her bed and unfolded the letter that smelled like Shawn's cologne. She smiled that he took the time to be so romantic and write a letter instead of sending her an email.

To My Joy,

I heard what you said last night, but I'm not giving up on us that easily. I know we've only known each other for a few months, but I can't imagine being without you. Your smile is like the sun, it warms me. We have such a great friendship and I can't imagine we wouldn't make a great couple. I mean, I'm smart and you're smart, and I'm good looking and you're good looking, and I've got a great sense of humor and you've got a great sense of humor, well, you get the point. We work. We'll be great together. Please give us a chance.

I don't know when you're going to read this letter, but please know that whatever day you open this, at whatever time, you will be on my mind. I got it bad for you. Please don't make me beg anymore. I can't wait to see you when break is over and you return to campus.
Your Boy,

Shawn

Joy read the letter like she needed the words to breathe. She held the letter to her chest when she finished, then danced around the room with excitement over how much Shawn liked her. She liked him, but that scared her. Joy wondered if she did fear loving someone because of her parents' failed marriage. She wondered if it was possible to let her guard down and open her heart to Shawn without hurting him or being hurt. Joy knew she had hurt Marley deeply and she didn't want to hurt anyone else, especially not her close friend. Yet everything Shawn said was true and Joy knew it. They would be great together. He made her smile. He made her laugh until she cried during their walks to class, all-night conversations on the phone, and weekly movie nights.

Joy resolved to pray about a relationship with Shawn and make a decision by the time she got back to campus.

While Joy prayed about what she should do, she also thought about Shawn a lot. It didn't help that they talked every day. If they didn't talk on the phone, they emailed each other. The night before Joy returned to campus, she read the letter one more time. She'd already read it at least thirty times since she'd been home for the week.

I'm going to give him a chance. I pray I won't regret it.

When Joy got back to campus, Shawn was waiting outside so he could take her bags to her apartment.

"I missed you, Noble." Shawn often called Joy by her last name. "Can I have a hug?"

"You can have more than that." Joy kissed him on the lips and on his chin.

"What do you mean?" Shawn pressed into Joy's body as she leaned against the wall, resting his head on her neck while he waited for a response.

"You can have me." Joy lifted Shawn's head from her shoulder, wrapping her arms around his neck. "That is, if you still want me."

"For real, sweetie?" Shawn hugged Joy and lifted her off the ground. "What changed your mind?" Shawn smiled from ear to ear as he set Joy back on the ground.

"You changed my mind. I love you as my friend and I'm ready

for that love to grow for you as my man. I pray you won't make me regret trusting you."

"Babe, you know you're in good hands."

From that night, Joy and Shawn were inseparable. In fact, Shawn halfway moved into Joy's apartment because he was there so much. He would go back to his apartment to play video games, shower, dress, and occasionally sleep. They also needed time apart once in a while, because spending every moment together was a recipe for arguments. They walked to class together, studied together, ate most of their meals together, and hung out together on the weekends.

Several nights during the week, Shawn would check his email at Joy's apartment. Joy noticed Shawn had a lot of female friends and she could tell some of them liked him. She wondered if Shawn had told any of them the same thing he was telling her. She wanted to make sure Shawn wasn't stringing her along, so she decided to read his email one night to see if he had any secrets.

Joy remembered Gran's warning against looking for trouble. She said bad news will always show up when it's sought. Gran was right. Joy got more than she bargained for when reading Shawn's email. She discovered he was talking to a female in their class, Tyra.

"Typical man. He doesn't know who he is messing with!" Joy said aloud to herself.

The next afternoon Shawn stopped by Joy's apartment like he always did. Joy decided to let him sit down before she started her interrogation. He turned on the television and sat in the chair closest to the front door. Shawn motioned Joy over to him, but she decided to sit across from him on the sofa.

"What's wrong with you?"

"Have you ever slept with Tyra?" Joy didn't have time for small talk. She was on a mission.

He looked puzzled by her question. "No."

"You're too calm for me. Have you ever talked about dating her?"

"Where is all this coming from?" Shawn leaned forward and rested his chin on his knuckles.

"I heard that you and Tyra had something going on," Joy persisted as she stood up. "I'm asking you if that's true."

"No, I never messed with Tyra. We did talk about dating each other and I admit I let that conversation go too far. I told her a few days ago I was seeing you."

"Why were you even talking about seeing someone else when we are seeing each other? Do you want to be with her instead of me?" she demanded with her arms folded.

"No, I don't." Shawn stood up quickly. "Who told you this?"

"You told me," Joy declared as she shook her head in disgust.

"What?" Shawn asked with a clueless look on his face.

"Get out." Joy opened the door and pointed Shawn to it so he would know she wanted him out.

Shawn stood in the doorway, still begging for an answer.

"Tell me who told you that."

"You told me when I read your email last night."

"You read what?" he yelled.

"I read your email." Joy rolled her neck. "You can't deny anything now."

"I can't believe you would do something like that to me. You had no right to read my email. I didn't do anything with Tyra. I guess I should have since you don't trust me."

Joy slammed the door in his face, forcing Shawn to back up before it hit him.

Joy was upset and confused. She ran to her room, threw herself across the bed, and cried. Arguing with Shawn made her heart ache and though she hadn't known him long, Joy couldn't imagine being happy without him. Still, if he was lying to her about Tyra, she had to let him go. She couldn't be with someone who would lie to her. She knew too well that the ruin of a relationship started with lies. She witnessed how Angel tolerated Lester's lies and she didn't want to play the fool. She was not going to be taken advantage of by anyone.

Soon after she threw herself onto the bed, her phone rang.

"Have you calmed down?" It was Shawn.

"A little." She sniffled.

"I have a few things to say, so please don't interrupt. I've never met anyone like you. You're intelligent, beautiful, funny, talented, and just fun to be with. I realize the gift you are and I would not play you. I will admit that a few days ago Tyra and I started emailing each other. It was innocent until she started talking about dating. Again, I admit the emails went too far at the time, but I recently told her I was seeing you, and she respected that. Then you go behind my back and read my email, my personal property. The fact that you invaded my privacy makes me question if I can trust you. Have you done that before?"

"No," she mumbled.

"I don't know where we stand now. It blows my mind that you would be that sneaky."

"Sneaky! That's harsh." Joy cringed as she felt the sting of that word.

"No, I think it's appropriate. You violated my trust, Joy. I'm shocked and hurt by your actions."

"I'm sorry. I know I didn't have the right to read your email. Do you forgive me?" Joy pleaded as she suddenly felt horrible about what she'd done to Shawn.

"I don't know. I have to think about it. I'll talk to you later." Shawn hung up the phone.

When Joy hung up she felt worse. The fate of their relationship was now out of her hands. That night she went to sleep without seeing or speaking to Shawn again. The next day Joy walked to the bus stop alone.

The first day Shawn refused to take Joy's calls or acknowledge her in public. She felt like someone had stabbed her in the heart repeatedly. The second day was even worse.

Joy timidly knocked on Shawn's apartment door with his favorite meal as a peace offering: a plate of chicken strips with rice. He didn't torment Joy and make her beg for his forgiveness.

"It took everything in me to ignore you for two days," he said when he opened the door.

$\cdot \ \cdot \ \cdot \ \cdot \ \cdot$

Joy treasured the time spent with Shawn discussing current events, business ideas, family, and marriage. He stimulated her with his intellect. Joy lived and breathed Shawn for months, so much so that at times she felt intoxicated. He gave her a natural high she'd never felt before. When Joy wasn't with him, she was thinking about him, about their future together. Joy had never dated a guy she envisioned marrying until Shawn. Joy would chat until the early morning with friends from home and undergrad about how happy she was with Shawn. They couldn't believe how hard she'd fallen for him in such a short time. Joy's friends always thought she would never fall head over heels in love with any guy because she always seemed to get bored with all her boyfriends. However, there was no doubt in Joy's mind that Shawn was the man she was going to marry. If he'd asked her to marry him, Joy would have replied with a resounding yes. She wanted to spend the rest of her life with him. She wanted to have his children. She wanted to be Mrs. Shawn Taylor.

In February Joy spent a lot of time thinking about love and forgiveness. Though she and Shawn were crazy about each other, they had their disagreements. There were times when Joy wanted to hold a grudge, but Shawn never wanted to keep an argument going. He always made the effort to make up.

With Valentine's Day approaching, Joy started thinking about her ideal romantic date. She was often disappointed in the past by dates or Valentine's Days that fell short of her imagination. Even though Joy knew what her ideal Valentine's Day would be like, she didn't give Shawn any hints because she wanted him to surprise her. On Valentine's Day, Joy decided to peek out her kitchen window to see what Shawn was doing at his apartment. She got excited watching him sneak balloons and bags out of his car. She watched him look over his shoulder, probably to make sure Joy wasn't spying on him. After watching him for a few minutes, she decided not to ruin his surprise and moved away from the window and got ready for class.

During class she thought about what Shawn was planning. Joy was so distracted she didn't scribble one note in her composition book during the entire two hours of Media Law class. Afterward, Joy waited at a friend's place for at least an hour and a half. It was eight o'clock when Shawn finally picked her up. He told Joy he had been running errands all afternoon.

When Shawn picked Joy up, he was out of breath. When Joy closed the car door she couldn't believe he had his windows rolled down.

"It's twenty degrees outside. Why do you have the windows rolled down, babe? Where have you been?"

Joy tried to interrogate Shawn about what was going on, but he refused to give her any clues. When they parked at Joy's apartment, he left her in the car, and ran up the steps like his feet were on fire.

Finally, Joy was allowed in her own apartment. When Shawn opened the door for her, Joy's eyes widened in amazement. The entire apartment was filled with short cream candles. The lights were dimmed and Jill Scott was playing softly. There were a dozen red long-stemmed roses in a vase on a small table covered with a white cloth. Behind the roses were red and pink balloons. Joy's kitchen table was moved into the living room and covered with a white linen tablecloth. There were two place settings and Chinese food boxes positioned perfectly on the table. There was also a bottle of sparkling cider and one red long-stemmed rose on the table for decoration.

Joy's mouth fell open in absolute awe. Shawn stood behind Joy and gently wrapped his arms around her waist and kissed her neck. Shawn pulled out the chair for Joy like they were at an expensive restaurant. The menu included all of her favorites.

"That's why the windows were rolled down, nosy. I didn't want you to smell the Chinese food I picked up a few minutes ago."

"Aw, you are too much, babe. Thank you." Joy began to tear up; nobody had ever done this for her.

"I've got some more surprises planned, poo, so please don't start crying now." Shawn smiled. "I hid your gifts in the apartment."

Joy walked around the living room, searching behind the television and sofa for a gift. She didn't find anything. Next, she looked behind the large floor fan and found a white battery-operated puppy.

"I remember this from the mall when we first started dating." Joy jumped with excitement as she stroked the toy pup's white fur.

Joy found the next gift hidden behind one of the sofa pillows. It was a Winnie-the-Pooh stuffed bear with a red heart between its arms. Winnie's heart read, *Be My Sweetie.*

"A Pooh for my poo."

At that moment, Joy was convinced Shawn was the only man she could ever love. There was no other man for her. He had a way of reading her mind and making things she could only dream of come true.

It was time for the last surprise, but Joy wanted to shower Shawn with gifts first. She went to the coat closet and pulled out a large red bag. In it were two cards, a stuffed tiger, a box of his favorite Hot Tamales candy, an artificial rose, and a pair of classic boxer shorts with red hearts. Pleased with his gifts, Shawn proceeded to turn the attention back to Joy.

She sat at the dining room table and closed her eyes.

Joy could hear Shawn fiddling with something in the kitchen. Per his request, she counted to five and opened her eyes. When she did, there was a chocolate raspberry cake in front of her. It was the same cake Joy told Shawn she wanted to try weeks earlier when they were grocery shopping.

"I love you."

They leaned across the table and shared a long, deep kiss. After dessert Shawn had one more thing on the agenda: Joy's favorite movie, *Love Jones.*

The Sunday after Valentine's Day, Joy went to church like she normally did with Ray, who lived in the apartment below her. The message was about fornication. It was not a new message, but as she listened to the preacher it was like he was talking directly to Joy. His eyes could have burned a hole in her forehead. Joy started to squirm in her seat. She knew that sleeping with someone who was not your spouse was a sin, but didn't think a relationship could last without being physically intimate. Throughout the school year, Joy would get sick, and she knew those illnesses were a physical manifestation of her guilt. Joy also knew she could not continue to profess Christ as her Lord and savior and willfully commit this sin. She was prepared to lose the love of her life for the man who loved Joy enough to die for her sins. Joy couldn't imagine life without Shawn, but she couldn't live without Jesus. At the end of the sermon when the invitation for being in a relationship with Jesus Christ, joining the church, or for prayers was extended, Joy walked to the altar and rededicated her life to Christ. She made a commitment to God that she would not have sex again until her wedding night and asked for forgiveness for being sexually active since high school.

"Hey, poo, what's up?" Shawn smiled and gave Joy a peck on the lips when she opened the door to her apartment.

"Hey, baby. Have a seat."

"What's wrong?" Shawn braced himself like something terrible was coming.

"Well, Shawn, you know I love you. You mean a lot to me. I can't believe that I've learned to love someone so much in such a short period of time. While I was so wrapped up in loving you, being with you, cooking for you, and being there for you, I forgot to be true to the most important man in my life."

"And who is the most important man in your life? Are you seeing somebody else?" Shawn questioned Joy like she was on a witness stand.

"No, I'm not seeing anyone else. Today in church I was reminded that I couldn't pretend like sleeping with you is not a sin. I love you, but I am not going to sleep with you anymore. I didn't make this decision just because it is wrong, but because I can't live with the guilt."

"Are you saying that you don't enjoy sleeping with me?" Shawn looked bewildered.

"No, I'm not saying that, but I'm saying that after you leave, I look at myself in the mirror and get sick. I would understand if you wouldn't want to be with me anymore. I know not having sex is a big sacrifice, but I am willing to make that sacrifice."

Shawn was silent for a few minutes. Joy wanted him to say something, anything.

"Joy, I knew you were a religious person when we met, and I have a relationship with God, too, though I'm not as dedicated to going to church and following the scripture as you. Even though you've never discussed this with me before, I sensed you carried some guilt about having sex. I also noticed you would never have sex with me on Sunday. I'm a Christian, too, and I understand where you are coming from. Honestly, I don't feel guilty about having sex and not being married because everyone has sex. The pastor who preached that message today fornicated. Our parents fornicated back in the day. My love for you is much deeper than sex. I do love sleeping with you, but I love talking to you more. I love spending time with you. I just love you and nothing is going to break us up. I know you are going to be my wife. I can wait until our wedding night to sleep with you again," Shawn assured her.

Joy couldn't believe her ears. She heard what Shawn said, but she didn't know if his restraint would last until they got married, though she was happy he was willing to wait for her.

CHAPTER TWENTY-FIVE

The first day of spring finally arrived, and more importantly it was Joy's birthday. To celebrate this annual occasion, Shawn took Joy to one of her favorite restaurants for dinner. After dinner, the waitress reappeared at their table and brought a slice of chocolate cake and five clapping employees with her. Joy was so embarrassed, while Shawn thought the entire performance was hilarious.

When they returned to Joy's apartment a few of their friends jumped out of the kitchen and screamed surprise. Shawn had invited them over for cake and ice cream. Shawn bought a sheet cake decorated with Winnie-the-Pooh and friends. It read, *Happy 23rd Birthday, Poo*. Joy thought Shawn was the best for always making her feel special. After everyone left, Shawn cleaned up the plates, cups, and leftover cake.

"Well, happy birthday again, sweetie. I guess I'll head over to my place for the night."

"Thanks for everything, babe. You are full of surprises. I love you." Joy kissed Shawn on the lips.

"I love you, too, poo. Don't forget a brotha when my birthday rolls around." Shawn laughed at his joke and hugged Joy goodnight.

Joy laughed as she shut the door behind him.

Shawn's birthday was a month after Joy's and she threw him a cookout to celebrate. Joy invited at least twenty of their classmates and friends to her apartment. Shawn operated the grill while Joy cooked everything else.

Later that night, while cleaning up the kitchen, Joy overheard a conversation about marriage between Shawn and their friend, Kelly.

"So where are you and Joy going to move when you get married?"

"I think California is a better place to raise a family than Maryland, but we haven't decided yet. I think I will be able to find a job anywhere, so we just have to decide where we want to move," Shawn answered.

Joy started smiling when she heard Shawn talking about marriage. Lately, all she ever thought about was being Shawn's wife and having his children. Joy was comforted to know that he thought about it, too.

Joy floated through the rest of the spring semester. Joy was so happy she hadn't thought much about the end of her last semester.

After a couple days, Joy noticed she hadn't spent as much time with Shawn. He hadn't stopped over like he normally did after class and he was calling less. One Saturday morning she decided to call Shawn and confront him about his behavior.

Shawn invited Joy to his apartment so they could talk. It was rare for them to be in his apartment because Shawn had a roommate. When Joy arrived at his apartment they hugged and he invited her in.

"Shawn, I know you too well. Are you okay?" Joy grabbed his hand, ready for whatever he had to say.

I wonder what's up with him. We seemed so happy and were inseparable, and now he wants to talk about something. Is he seeing someone else? He couldn't be. He wouldn't do that to me. But what else could it be? Normally, I'm the one who starts being distant to get rid of someone, not the other way around.

"Poo, you do know me well. Please sit down next to me." Shawn tapped the space on the sofa where he wanted Joy to sit.

"This is very hard for me to say, but I need you to let me say this without interruption."

"You are scaring me with the lead-ins and disclaimers, but I will let you finish." Joy started fiddling with her fingers in anticipation of what he was going to say.

"Joy, I love you with all my heart. I know I've been distant the past few days. Reason being, it hit me that the end of the semester is approaching and I'll be moving back to Cali and you'll be moving back to B-more. Neither one of us has secured jobs yet, so we can't afford to move. I don't want to add the extra strain of a long-distance relationship to our lives." Shawn grabbed Joy's hand, so she would stop fidgeting.

"What are you saying, Shawn?" Joy fiddled with her fingers and tapped her foot as it seemed like an eternity before Shawn spoke again.

"I want us to break up until we can live in the same state."

"But I love you and I thought you loved me." Joy bawled on Shawn's shoulder until she could gain her composure. "I don't want us to be apart, but if this is what you want then I will go peacefully." Joy stood up and headed for the front door.

"Poo, why do you have to be so dramatic? This is not the end for us," Shawn promised.

"Well, it's certainly not the beginning, is it?" Joy said with the little sarcasm she could muster.

"What does that mean?" Shawn stood up to be closer to Joy.

"It means you convinced me to give you a chance and I did. Now I'm in love with you and you're letting me go and giving me some bogus excuse." Joy folded her arms, drained from the conversation.

"What's bogus about it? We are going to be living on two different sides of the map. How can we be in a relationship?"

"We are in love, so why wouldn't we try to make it? But if you want to part ways, let's start now. It's been a great year and I wish you the best." Joy extended her hand to Shawn like she was closing a business deal.

"Why does it have to be all or nothing? We started as friends, fell in love, and I want us to stay in touch until we can be together."

"This hurts so much because I opened my heart to you, and now I'm heartbroken." Joy left Shawn's apartment crying as she walked across the lawn to her place.

Shawn watched her walk away and hoped she would understand he was not trying to hurt her, but being practical.

After the breakup Joy tried to stop thinking about Shawn. It was too painful to be in his presence, so she did everything in her power to avoid him.

Shawn stopped by Joy's apartment one night to talk things out.

"Joy, we have shared so much. I don't want us to leave angry with one another. We are going to survive this break." Shawn seemed confident about the outcome.

"Maybe. Shawn, we have been through a lot and no matter what happens, I'm glad I fell in love with you. At least I know that kind of love is possible for me. Give me a hug." Joy smiled and remembered all the wonderful things they'd shared and all the things she'd learned.

Shawn and Joy spent all of their time together the last few days of the summer semester. The night before Joy's family arrived to move her back to Baltimore, she wrote Shawn a letter. In it, Joy told him how much he meant to her, and that he was responsible for one of the best years of her life. Before Shawn, Joy thought she wasn't capable of being in love. After him, Joy realized she could be in love and give someone her all without being afraid. In the letter Joy also revealed she prayed that God would reunite them soon. She placed a picture of both of them inside the envelope and sealed it with a Hershey's Kiss.

The next morning Shawn helped transport Joy's things into the moving truck. Angel thought Shawn seemed like a nice guy, but didn't think it was that serious, since he hadn't made plans to move to Maryland after they graduated.

While her family was working, Joy and Shawn would sneak

kisses. When the last box was loaded on the truck, they gathered in the apartment and prayed for a safe journey home.

Joy's family headed for the truck and left Shawn and Joy to say their goodbyes.

"I got something for you." Joy gave Shawn a letter she wrote.

"Is it dirty?"

"Shut up! You are a fool!" Joy laughed. "Read it and find out."

"I'll read it later."

"I'm going to miss you, babe." Joy held back the tears as she kissed Shawn softly on the lips.

"Poo, please stop talking like we are never going to see each other again. We'll be together before you know it. I promise." Shawn embraced Joy tightly.

When Joy's family started honking the horn, she and Shawn locked up her apartment and walked down the steps together for the last time.

CHAPTER TWENTY-SIX

As soon as Joy arrived at home she called Shawn. She told him about the uneventful trip and how she thought about him the entire ride home. By that time, Joy expected Shawn to be on a layover to California, but he said he had missed his flight. Shawn shared that once Joy left he read the letter she wrote him and sulked around his apartment, and as a result missed his flight.

At the conclusion of their call, Joy lay in bed for hours thinking about Shawn. Their first year together had been amazing, and she hoped the distance between them wouldn't negate everything they'd been through. Uncertain of the future of their relationship, Joy started unpacking. At two in the morning, Joy was still awake. It was at this hour she did a lot of soul searching. She hadn't spoken to Lester her entire year of graduate school. He never called to ask how she was or even to wish her a happy birthday. There were times Joy went days without thinking about him. It was almost like he was dead. The only difference was that Joy couldn't mourn.

On the other hand, there were mornings she would think about Lester. She would think about how much she looked up to him as a child. Joy thought about how he made her feel safe growing up. She remembered the times they went to professional wrestling matches or when he took her to see the musical *Dream Girls*. Joy wondered what happened to the man she once respected and admired.

She wondered if Lester thought about her. Joy pondered what hindered him from still being her father. Lester ruined his marriage and hurt his children, but to Joy it didn't seem like he wanted to repair the relationships he'd destroyed. Joy started praying that she would have a heart to forgive him. It would be a painful journey, but if she was going to love without limitation, Joy had to release what she was hiding behind.

· · · · ·

Before Joy tackled her relationship issues with Lester, she had to address something else immediately. Her first assignment was to get a job. She sent out dozens of resumes every week and was shocked when not one of the applications she mailed prompted a response. Joy thought getting a job would be easy since she had a master's degree. However, she learned that in a terrible economy a master's only meant Joy had the right to stand in the unemployment line with everyone else. Weeks passed and she was still unemployed without any job prospects. Joy tried not to be disappointed, because she knew God hadn't brought her through school to be jobless.

A couple months passed and Joy became discouraged. Her heart was broken. She had no money and hadn't been on an interview since moving back home. Joy was looking for something, but she couldn't articulate exactly what she was seeking. It wasn't the obvious, like a job, or being back with Shawn, but it was something else. She prayed God would show her what to do next. Joy had seen God move in her life, and she was confident that He knew what was best for her. Joy continued to apply for jobs and network while at home. She also spent a lot of time with her family, which always made her feel better.

At one of their family gatherings, one of Joy's cousins talked about the church he joined and invited everyone to visit on Sunday. Moses, Joy, and a few of their cousins had to see what all the excitement was about, so they planned to attend service the following Sunday.

They went to the eleven o'clock service, amazed at all the

young people gathered at church. The worship service was like no other. The music had Joy on her feet the entire time, and the preaching made her jump because it seemed the pastor spoke directly to her. Joy felt so invigorated by the service she planned to attend the following Sunday. The church was only a few years old and was one of the fastest growing African Methodist Episcopalian (AME) churches on the East Coast. The pastor was a dynamic preacher, in his mid-thirties, and delivered a sermon in a way that was exciting and relatable to Joy and her peers. Joy was rejuvenated after service and encouraged that she would find a job and be reunited with Shawn.

Shawn and Joy talked less as the months passed. He said it was because his phone bill was too high, but Joy thought he was weaning himself away from her. Joy was hurt that he didn't pursue her with the passion he once did, but she still held onto the promise he made.

In February, Joy interviewed with the largest newspaper in Maryland, *Charm City*. She did some freelance writing for them a few times, and the editor was so impressed with her work she sent Joy's resume to human resources. It was a blessing that a features writer position became available. A week after the interview, the features editor called and offered Joy the position. Overwhelmed with excitement, Joy ran up and down all the steps in her house screaming, "I'm employed! God is so faithful!"

Joy loved writing for the paper. Even though she worked long hours on stories and didn't make a lot of money, she didn't mind because it was her passion. Not to mention, all the work kept her mind on something other than Shawn.

Spring arrived and Shawn's calls were more sporadic. Joy tried to date other guys, but that just made her miss Shawn more. Even Angel set Joy up on a few blind dates, but they were all disasters. No man could make Joy feel the way Shawn did. He was her best friend and soul mate.

"Joy, I think you're too picky," Angel said as she poked her head in Joy's bedroom one evening.

"Shouldn't you be picky about the person you are going to

spend the rest of your life with?" Joy looked up from lying on her pillow facedown. She was listening to some of Mary J. Blige's saddest songs when Angel interrupted.

"Yes, but you weed the guys out before you give them a chance." Angel shook her head and sat on Joy's bed. "Like the guy from my church. There was nothing wrong with him and in one date you wrote him off."

"He was boring. All he did was talk about how smart he is and quoted Bible scriptures the entire night."

"Joy, you need to forget about Shawn. I'm telling you this because I care. If he had planned to be with you, he would have moved here for you." Angel gave Joy a hug and left her to listen to the sad love songs alone.

It seemed that Angel wasn't the only one who wanted Joy to forget about Shawn. Joy's friends agreed and tried to cheer her up, but nothing worked. They took her to poetry venues, but that only inspired her to write poems about Shawn. Joy read some of her poems for open mic night and had the audience in tears when she left the stage.

No matter what Joy did she thought about Shawn. Even her attempt at being angry with him failed.

On Joy's birthday, she got a phone call around five p.m. The sound of Shawn's voice sent chills up her spine. Joy wanted to leap with excitement when she heard from him, but pretended to be calm.

"Happy birthday, poo. I miss you," Shawn said in his sexy voice.

"Hi, baby, I miss you, too. I haven't heard from you in a while." Joy couldn't stop grinning.

"Poo, I just talked to you last week."

"Was that last week? It seemed longer." The doorbell sounded. "Hold on, somebody is at my door. I'm going to keep the phone to my ear, so I can soak up every moment of this conversation."

"Okay, I guess I should keep talking to you, so you can soak me up." Shawn laughed.

When Joy opened the door, Shawn was standing in the walkway with a dozen long-stemmed roses and a sign: *Guess Who Got a Job in B-More?*

Joy threw the phone on the floor, jumped up and down, and screamed in the doorway like she'd just won a million dollars. Then she ran outside and jumped in Shawn's arms, knocking the sign out of his hand. They must have kissed a hundred times. Joy couldn't get enough of touching his soft lips with hers. She tried to stop, but missed him too much to even come up for air.

"Still think I don't miss you?" Shawn asked as he held Joy close.

"I love you so much." She laid her head against his and smiled.

"I love you more."

For Joy, life was too good. She had a great job and the love of her life had left his home to be closer. It didn't get any better than this.

CHAPTER TWENTY-SEVEN

Shawn and Joy talked often about marriage and how they planned to save for their wedding. They decided it would be best if Joy stayed at home with Angel, while Shawn moved in with his cousin Stan. Doing this would help them save for the wedding without living together, which they decided was not an option.

In March, the same month Shawn moved to Baltimore, Joy subscribed to *Modern Bride* magazine and began browsing bridal websites every other day.

"Joy, you may want to slow down about being married," Angel said as Joy sat in the dining room looking at bridesmaids' dresses in a magazine.

"Why should I slow down when we are in love? He moved here to be with me." Joy shook her head, thinking Angel was trying to rain on her parade.

"Joy, don't shake your head at me. I'm happy for you, but Shawn just moved here and you two aren't engaged yet. So I'm just saying continue to pray about being married to him and calm down just a little." Angel stood behind Joy and hugged her from behind.

"I can't calm down, Mom. I'm excited. I mean, before you were telling me I'm too picky and pointing out that Shawn hadn't moved here. Now he's moved and we are together and you're telling me to calm down. I can't win," Joy said as she flipped the pages of the magazine.

"All I'm saying is I don't want you to make the same mistake I did. Pray about it and let things progress. When he proposes, then start planning the wedding. Just some motherly advice."

"Unsolicited advice." Joy laughed.

"That's the best kind of advice a mother can give," Angel said, then went in the kitchen and left Joy with her bridal magazine.

When Joy wasn't planning the wedding, she was talking to Shawn about wedding plans. Shawn mentioned he wanted to meet Lester. He said something about formally asking him for her hand in marriage.

"You don't need to ask him. He doesn't even know me anymore. Just ask my mother if you want to be formal," Joy said in one very quick breath like she wanted to blow the idea out of Shawn's mind.

"I am going to ask your mother, but I want to ask your father, too. I at least want to meet him, Joy."

Joy had already decided that Moses would give her away at the wedding ceremony. She would send Lester an invitation, but figured he probably wouldn't come. Shawn insisted on meeting Lester and he encouraged Joy to improve her relationship with him as well.

Nine months passed and Joy still hadn't talked to or seen Lester. In January, Joy received a letter with Lester's name and a Maryland post office box number in the return address section. Joy wondered what he wanted. She held the envelope in shock, almost numb. Though she anxiously wanted to rip open the letter to see how Lester explained where he'd been, Joy carefully opened the envelope as not to damage the contents, and inside was a one-page, handwritten letter.

Dear Joy,

Happy Holidays! I am currently enrolled in a drug treatment inpatient 28-day program. I'm making an honest attempt to get my life together. I realize that much work has to be done and I am committed to doing it. One of the first things the counselors suggested I do is right some wrongs. There are several things wrong with our relationship. It is fractured, broken, we really don't have one. With your help, I would like very much to correct our relationship. At the very least, I would like for us to show mutual concern for one another. I apologize for all that I have not been. I am asking you to help me regain the love and respect of a daughter that I am very proud of. Please give this idea of forgiveness some prayerful consideration.

Love,

Dad

Joy read the first line of the letter over and over again. *He's in a drug treatment center? My father is in a drug treatment center? My father is a drug addict?* She stared at the letter for a while, trying to digest what it meant. She was repulsed that Lester was a drug addict, but also felt relieved because she now understood the reason he left. There was now a tangible reason for his lies. There was no excuse for stealing from your child, but now Joy understood. He was suffering from a sickness.

Joy wondered what else Lester did to get high. She wondered if he'd robbed or killed for drugs. She pictured the junkies that staggered up and down the streets of Baltimore City. Joy wondered if he was one of the people who got high in abandoned buildings or in alleys. Joy couldn't believe that the smart, strong man she once knew had become the victim of drug addiction. Joy wondered when he started using drugs and what drove him to it.

Joy ran upstairs to Angel's room and read the letter to her.

"You don't look surprised."

"I've known for a long time your father had a drug problem." Angel sighed like she was reliving her past with Lester.

"We were arguing about finances one day and he slipped and told me he had stopped using drugs. I guess he thought I knew.

He promised that he was going to get a job and stay clean, but that was the beginning of the end for him," Angel confided.

"I can't believe this. When did he tell you about the drugs?"

"About ten years ago."

"Ten years. Why didn't you say anything?"

"What would I say to my children? That your father had a drug problem? I could never ruin the image of your father for you and Moses." Angel sat next to Joy on the bed and held her hands. "That's not what a mother does, or at least not me. I would rather hide it from you and let you find out the truth on your own."

"But that would have answered some questions about why Dad started acting so crazy," Joy said as she let go of Angel's hands and picked the letter up off the bed.

"You wouldn't have felt any better knowing. I knew and it still hurt. Your father was such a smart man with so much potential. To see him throw everything away and knowing the reason why didn't ease the pain." Angel put her arm around Joy's shoulders. "Do you feel better knowing?"

"I don't feel better, but I feel enlightened," Joy said as she stood up, grabbed the letter, and went downstairs.

While downstairs, she peeked into Moses's old room. Since he moved out, Angel put any mail that came to the house for him on the dresser so he could pick it up when he visited. Joy wondered if he got a letter too. She didn't see anything on his dresser or on his bed, but as she closed the door she saw the letter balled up in his trashcan.

Joy understood Moses's rage toward Lester, but she didn't want to throw her letter away. Joy wanted to write him back.

One afternoon, Joy sat at her desk and thought about everything Lester had been to her, the good and all the bad. She reminisced about so many things. She laughed and cried, then poured her heart into the letter she sent to Lester.

The next week Joy received another letter from Lester. It had a different tone than the first one. The first message was humble and seemed to seek amends. The second letter was quite different.

Dear Joy,

The reason I walked out of your life was because your mother kicked me out. It has always been my desire to be a father to you. I've made some mistakes, but nobody is perfect. The times I saw you in passing years ago, you acted like you didn't want to be bothered. As a Christian, you should not bring up what happened, but move on and forgive. In fact, you should forget everything and we should be able to pick up like nothing ever happened. I ask you to consider this and of course pray about it.

The reason I started using was because I couldn't forgive myself for not taking care of my youngest son. You may have been too young to remember this, but remember when we took care of a little boy for a few weeks shortly after we moved into the house? His name was Jacob. In anger, shame, and out of hatred for his mother, I decided not to be there for him. It made me sick that I allowed him to grow up without a father, like I did. I tried to find out how he was doing over the past couple years, and I was told he's been in and out of jail since his freshman year of high school. I guess I'm to blame, because I didn't show him a better way.

I heard through the grapevine that you are going to be getting married and as your father, I should walk you down the aisle. I hope to meet this man you are supposed to be marrying soon.
Love,

Dad

"Who does he think he is? I'm going to let him know exactly what I think," Joy said out loud.

Dear Dad,

I hope you are progressing well in your program. I think

every good relationship is built upon honesty. I can only be honest in my response to you. I hope you will receive this with a clear mind and heart.

As I stated in the first letter I sent to you, I have already forgiven you because I love you and am a Christian. Over the past few years I have learned and experienced a lot. Those experiences have caused me to grow as a person and as a Christian. I was disappointed by some of your comments in the second letter you sent me. When I received the first letter it seemed like you were sincere about putting your life back together and making amends. In the second letter, however, you made it seem as if you deserve my forgiveness, that I should forget everything you've done and act like you are the best father in the world.

It is a wonderful thing that God forgives us instantly and wipes the slate clean when we confess our sins, but he still holds us accountable. I do forgive you and I don't intend to hold any of your previous actions over your head. At the same time, I can't honestly say I can forget those things. If you expect us to pick up our relationship when it was good, without going through the process of getting to know each other again, I can't do that. I don't know you anymore. I do want you in my life but I don't think this will or should happen overnight.

If you are committed to improving and making amends, I don't see how that is possible without confronting your past. You said that you forgave your father and loved him with all your heart. That's great. You also said he was the best father he could be, but I'm not buying that. I think being the best father you can be is always being there for your children. Even though you forgave your father and loved him, it was apparent that you had not forgotten how he'd hurt you.

I remember a conversation we had a while ago when you told me you never wanted to be like your father. You shared that after you told me about the Christmas your father bought presents and gave them to his girlfriend's children while you and Aunt Reese didn't receive anything. I don't think your recollection of the negative things about your father means you love him any less, but it does mean those memories exist.

I am aware Mom asked you to leave that night and that she threatened to call the police. I had been eavesdropping at the bottom of the steps. I also know that my telling her of the confrontation I had with your mistress the night before finally sent her over the edge and caused her to put you out. I was relieved the night you left and have remained relieved every day since. I was unhappy with your lifestyle and the drama it brought into our home. When you left, it was finally over.

I pray that as you ask for forgiveness, you will accept it humbly and not with the attitude that you deserve it. That will only push people away. I pray that your recovery goes well. I hope my honesty does not cause you to regress in your quest for making amends.

So I have a half-brother. I remember those weeks Jacob stayed with us. I feel for him and I pray he will be able to turn his life around. I would like to meet him one day.

Oh, I wanted to let you know that I bumped into Mr. Peterson the other day. He told me that it was because of you that he accepted Jesus Christ as his savior. He told me that many people, especially young men, were impacted by your ministry. He thanks God for you and told me to tell you that your preaching was not in vain.

Joy

Joy felt free. She sprung up from her desk like a weight had been lifted off her shoulders. In the letter, Joy said everything she wanted to say to Lester and breathed in and exhaled like she could move on with Shawn, leaving the pain of her past behind.

She told Shawn about the letters between her and Lester. Joy also assured Shawn she would pray about her relationship with

Lester and how they should move forward. She promised Shawn if Lester called or sent his number in a letter, there was a good chance they could meet.

A couple weeks later, Lester was released from the treatment center and called Joy. He wanted to meet Shawn as soon as possible and Joy obliged. Joy made dinner reservations for seven. She invited Moses, his live-in girlfriend/mother of his two children, Shawn, and Lester. Lester told Joy he was bringing two surprise guests.

Moses and Lester weren't on good terms, but Moses was not a mean person, so he could go to dinner, laugh, and remain calm like he never had an issue with Lester. Lester had never met Moses's two sons, Morgan and Mason.

Angel called Moses weekly, asking him when he was going to marry his girlfriend, Jessica. Angel would always end the conversation with the scripture reference, it is better to marry than to burn. However, Moses decided years ago that he would never get married and he made that clear to Jessica. He thought marriage was a means to force people to stay in relationships. He felt people should have the freedom to leave if they were unhappy. Moses also thought marriage was nothing more than a meaningless piece of paper and couldn't understand why anyone would willingly do it. He and Jessica were happy and he loved being a father, so for him, they were better off than most married couples.

They decided to meet at a quaint Italian restaurant in Baltimore County for dinner. Joy and Shawn arrived first and were seated, followed by Moses and Jessica. The couples made small talk while they waited for Lester and his guests.

"I wonder who Dad is bringing with him. Maybe he has to bring along a mediator from the rehabilitation program to make sure things go smoothly," Joy said while tapping her fingers on the wooden table like she was solving a mystery.

"Here we go with Detective Noble trying to figure everything out all the time. Can't you just wait like everyone else to see who the mystery guests are?" Shawn shook his head and laughed at Joy's curiosity.

"Looks like we don't have to wait any longer," Moses said as Lester walked in with his guests.

"I don't believe it! What is going on?" Joy said as she rose from her chair.

When Lester arrived, he looked healthier than they'd seen him in a while. He had gained some weight and his white hair had a luster that made him look distinguished. He was well-dressed and accompanied by Angel and a young man nobody knew, but seemed very familiar to Joy and Moses.

"Mom, what are you doing here with Dad?" Joy asked before Angel barely sat down.

"Let's all sit down so I can explain why I'm here, but before that let's do some introductions," Angel said. "Lester, this is Shawn, Joy's soon-to-be fiancé. This is Jessica, Moses's girlfriend and the mother of our beautiful grandsons. Last, but not least, everyone this is Jacob, Joy and Moses's half-brother."

"Whoa! What? I didn't see that one coming. I have a brother. Did you know about this, Joy?" Moses asked as he sized Jacob up.

"Oh yeah, I guess you didn't read the letters Dad wrote you. I thought I mentioned it to you a few weeks ago," Joy said.

"No, I'm sure that's a conversation I would have remembered." Moses rolled his eyes at Joy because they had talked about so many other things over the past few weeks, but not once did Joy mention Jacob.

"Nice meeting you, Jacob. I hope we can spend some time together and get to know you," Joy said.

"I would like that," Jacob said as he hugged Joy and gave Moses some dap.

Jacob and Moses looked like they could be twins; the striking resemblance was shocking. The two young men were spitting images of Lester when he was in his twenties. The only difference was that their complexions were a few shades lighter than Lester's. Moses and Jacob were both six-feet three-inches tall, with a medium build. Jacob also seemed quiet like Moses.

"So let's order some appetizers and get to the bottom of why

Mom is here with Dad," Joy said as she pulled her chair closer to the table.

"Well, while your father was writing you two letters, he was also writing to me and I decided to write back. I didn't share this with either of you because I wanted you to decide for yourselves how you would respond to his request to make amends. I've forgiven him, and my desire is for your father and I to be friends. We've known each other for almost twenty-eight years and brought you two into the world. The least we can do is channel all of that love and experience into a friendship. So when he asked me to come tonight, I thought it would be a great start at celebrating Joy and Shawn's pending engagement as a family," Angel said.

"Angel, I appreciate you coming tonight and I am overwhelmed by your forgiveness. I know I've written all of you letters, trying to build our relationships again, but I want to say to all of you I apologize. I truly regret all the pain I've caused each of you and I realize it can't be reversed, but I do pray for reconciliation. I've been clean for some months now and I've started applying for jobs. I'm living with your Aunt Reese while I get back on my feet. I've also been studying the Word and I'm thankful we serve the God of another chance. Though I've messed up, I'm still here and I'm a recipient of His grace and mercy," Lester said.

"I would like to say something," Jacob said.

Everyone stopped talking and moving when Jacob spoke. He had been quiet for most of the night, so he had their attention.

"It hurt not knowing my father growing up, especially because my stepfather seemed to hate me so much, but I'm not going to continue to be mad at the world. I forgive you, and I want you to be in my life."

By this time, Joy was bawling in a wad of Kleenex. She was flooded with emotion as she thought about the good and bad times she shared with her family.

"Dad, I forgive you, and I pray we can all move forward. I know it will be a process, but I'm willing to try," Joy said as she blew her nose. "What about you, Moses?"

"Should we vote on it?" Moses asked, grinning. "Well, since it looks like I'm outnumbered, welcome back to our lives, Dad. Can we order some food now?"

"Right after we finish introductions. Hi, Jessica, nice to meet you. I would like to spend some time with my grandsons."

Jessica smiled. "Sure."

Lester turned to Shawn. "I hear you want to marry my daughter. If you hurt her, I'll break your neck. Nice to meet you."

"Nice meeting you, too, Mr. Noble. I hope the guys can hang out so I can talk to you about a few things," Shawn said.

Joy couldn't believe how quickly things had changed. One moment she didn't know where Lester was, and now she was at dinner with him. She marveled at how awesome God was and how He reunited her family before Shawn proposed. Joy prayed the worst of times was behind them.

CHAPTER TWENTY-EIGHT

J oy was turning twenty-five and didn't want a big party, just to
spend time with Shawn. He'd been acting secretive lately and
Joy wanted to make sure nothing was bothering him. The morning of her birthday, Shawn called while she was driving to the
hairdresser.

"Hey, poo."

"I love when you say that. Hey, baby, what's up?"

"Happy birthday, sexy."

"Thank you." Joy blushed.

"I want to take you to dinner tonight, so meet me at the restaurant. I have to go to work for a few hours." Shawn sounded
slightly disappointed.

"Okay, what restaurant?"

"The Olive Twig."

"You are so simple," Joy said, laughing. "It's the Olive Garden."

"Twig, branch, garden—what difference does it make?"
Shawn's laugh was strong and sexy. Hearing it always warmed
Joy's heart.

"What time, silly?" Joy was still grinning.

"Meet me there at seven."

"Okay, sounds good."

"Oh," Shawn said that like he was forgetting something
important. "Wear the black dress I bought you."

"What black dress?"

"The one I gave to your mother to hide at the house for your birthday."

"You think you are so slick. I love you," Joy sang loudly.

"Why are you so loud?" Shawn held the phone away from his ear. "I love you more. See you at the restaurant."

Joy spent the entire morning and most of the afternoon being pampered. After getting her hair done she went to the nail salon and got a manicure and pedicure. Her cell phone rang the entire time, with birthday wishes from family and friends. When she left the nail salon, Joy went home and rested until it was time to get ready for the dinner date.

Shawn was normally late, so she took her time getting ready. She arrived at the restaurant at 7:15. Joy told the hostess the reservation was in Shawn's name and she escorted her to the private dining area in the rear of the restaurant.

Why is she taking me back here? Joy wondered.

When Joy walked into the room, she couldn't see anything because it was pitch black.

"What's going on?" Joy asked the hostess.

Before she could respond, the light flicked on and a room full of friends and family cheered and clapped.

"Surprise!"

In front of the crowd was Shawn.

"Happy birthday, poo. You are a sexy old woman."

"I got your old woman." Joy beamed. "Give me a birthday kiss."

"My pleasure." Shawn's smile alone could have lit the room.

As they kissed, the room filled with claps and cheers. Joy walked around and greeted all the guests. She couldn't believe that Shawn's mother, Ms. Deon, flew in from California just for her birthday.

All of Joy's friends from home were there and even some from Orange University. Nearly her entire family was in attendance, including Lester. When the excitement dwindled, everyone sat and ate dinner. They reminisced and talked about current events during dinner. Naturally, Shawn felt the need to tell jokes.

After dinner someone yelled, "Cut the cake." Shawn escorted Joy to the cake table while everyone else joined in singing "Happy Birthday." When Joy sang her last note of how old she was now, Shawn interrupted.

"I want to thank all of you for coming. Joy is a special woman and I know she means a lot to everyone in this room. Before we cut the cake I have something important to say."

Shawn took Joy's hand and said, "This gathering is not just a birthday celebration, but a demonstration of my love for you. Joy, you are the best thing that ever happened to me. Your beauty, intelligence, spirituality, strength, and love inspire me to be a better man. I don't want to live another day without you by my side. I am in love with you and I want to love you for the rest of our lives."

While Shawn was talking, Joy started sweating and getting anxious.

When she looked at Shawn she saw Lester. She started thinking about how horrible her parents' marriage ended and she didn't want that to happen to her and Shawn. She thought about the lies and the broken promises, the infidelity and abuse.

Shawn knelt down on one knee and pulled out a tiny black box. When he opened it, the diamond blinded Joy.

"Joy Marie Noble, will you marry me?"

Everyone stared and waited for Joy's response, but she couldn't open her mouth. People started whispering in the background.

"Joy, did you hear me? What's wrong?"

Joy pulled her hand away from Shawn's and gave him an apologetic look. "I'm sorry."

She grabbed her purse and ran out of the dining room.

"Joy, Joy, Joy!" Shawn screamed.

She couldn't go back. Joy ran out of the restaurant toward her car. When she turned around, Shawn was running after her. Joy kept running until she reached her car. Then she pulled off and raced home.

When she arrived at home, Joy sat in the car with her head on the steering wheel. Her cell phone rang relentlessly. She felt terrible. The only thing Joy wanted more than the air she breathed was to be Shawn's wife. However, at that moment, all she thought to do was escape.

"I'm so embarrassed. Shawn threw a party for me and I ran out on him, our friends, and our family," Joy cried out.

When Joy finally made it in the house, she locked herself in her room. She stretched out across the bed and cried herself to sleep in the dark. She woke up to banging on her bedroom door at six a.m.

"Joy, open the door," Angel demanded.

"I don't want to talk to anyone."

"Why did you run out last night? Shawn was heartbroken. Why would you hurt him like that?"

"I didn't mean to."

Joy opened the door and fell into Angel's arms.

"I didn't mean to run out, but I got scared. What if I can't love someone for the rest of my life? What if Shawn cheats on me?"

"Joy, you can't live your life based on what-ifs. I know Shawn loves you and you love him. The rest is up to the both of you. I have something to share with you. I was going to wait until you accepted Shawn's proposal last night, but with you running out it never happened."

"What do you have to tell me?" Joy looked perplexed.

"I'm engaged." Angel flashed her engagement ring and smiled.

"To who?"

"A guy at my church has been courting me for the past six months. You've been so busy with Shawn you didn't notice how busy my social life has been lately. Anyway, I prayed about it when he initially asked me to go out with him and God showed me clearly that this man is my husband. I never thought I would get married again, but I am so happy and I know you and Shawn will be happy, too. If I can forgive and love again, so can you. Please call Shawn. He has already called several times this morning."

"I will, but I have to go somewhere first," Joy said tearfully.

Joy wanted to go to the one place that held all the answers.

After she took a shower and got dressed, Joy drove to church. It was close to her house; she needed to go there for clarity. She remembered hearing that the doors of the church were always open. *Let's see if that's true,* Joy thought as she approached the parking lot.

There were a handful of cars in the lot when she parked, but Joy knocked on the door, hoping someone would let her in.

"Can I help you?" an older gentleman asked.

"I just want to go to the altar and pray. Is that all right?"

"I don't see why not."

When she entered the quiet, dimly lit sanctuary, it felt even more sacred than it did during Sunday-morning service. Joy went to the altar and knelt.

"Dear Heavenly Father, I'm scared. I need your help to be the wife I know I can be. Please confirm that Shawn and I won't end up like my parents. I don't know what else to say, but please speak to me. I'm going to stay here until your word is clear. In Jesus's name I pray, Amen."

Joy lost track of time while kneeling there, and when she looked up there was a tiny black box sitting on the altar. She was shocked that God had given her such a clear sign. When she turned around and saw Shawn, she knew then the box hadn't fallen from Heaven, but was still a miracle.

"I knew you would be here. At least I prayed I would find you here."

"Shawn, I'm sorry." Joy stood from kneeling at the altar.

"Joy, I want you to listen to me. I know your father hurt you and your family, but I'm not him. I will never lie to you. I will never cheat on you. I will never hit you. I love you. I know I'm not perfect, but I can try to love you perfectly. I want you to step out on faith and be my bride."

Shawn got down on one knee and opened the tiny black box again. "Joy Marie Noble, will you marry me?"

"Shawn, I can't believe I ran out on you last night. There's nothing that would make me happier than being your wife, but when you asked at the restaurant, all of these emotions I didn't realize were hidden in my heart overwhelmed me and I was afraid. I know you're a good man and I love you."

Shawn reached up and gently wiped the tears streaming down Joy's cheeks with the back of his hand. Still kneeling on one knee, he waited for Joy's answer.

"Yes."